THE ELDER ICE

DAVID HAMBLING

Contents

Visit the Shadows from Norwood Facebook page –
https://www.facebook.com/ShadowsFromNorwood
for links, photographs, interactive map and more about this
series

For PRJH

Norwood, South London, 1924

This may seem fanciful to the reader, but the impression was real to us at the time. People living under civilised conditions, surrounded by Nature's varied forms of life and by all the familiar work of their own hands, may scarcely realise how quickly the mind, influenced by the eyes, responds to the unusual and weaves about it curious imaginings like the firelight fancies of our childhood days.

Ernest Shackleton, *South: The Story of Shackleton's 1914-1917 Expedition*

The People of the Eastern Ice, they are melting like the snow—
They beg for coffee and sugar; they go where the white men go.

The People of the Western Ice, they learn to steal and fight;
They sell their furs to the trading-post: they sell their souls to the
white.

The People of the Northern Ice, they trade with the whaler's crew;
Their women have many ribbons, but their tents are torn and few.

But the People of the Elder Ice, beyond the white man's ken—
Their spears are made of the narwhal-horn, and they are the last of
the Men!

- Rudyard Kipling, *The Jungle Book*

PROLOGUE

IT WILL BE CONVENIENT TO state here the details of an incident of which I was unaware until much later.

It happened that late one evening, a man called Waters staggered into the Greyhound public house in Sydenham. He was well known there, and the occupants of the pub naturally assumed Waters already in drink. Barely coherent, he had to lean on the bar for support. He was in a state of some distress and saying the devil was after him. At first his listeners laughed, assuming some drunken, comical misidentification had occurred and suggesting his devil had been either a donkey or a dustman.

Then they saw the trickles of blood running from under his hat. They crowded round and persuaded Waters to stand still while one of the men took off his hat, stiff with blood, to inspect the injury.

The back of Waters' head came off with it.

Waters slumped over, dead as a doornail, and dark, sticky gore spattered the witnesses. The landlady screamed and fainted dead away. Paralysis struck an elderly man who was later taken to hospital.

All of the witnesses agreed that the sudden and unnatural death was a sight of unutterable horror. They struggled to describe it to the police and preferred not to discuss it afterwards. Those hardened by the War said the death in that cosy pub was worse than the trenches.

The pub was closed the next week, and the week after. After that, they shut it down. The landlady, who had been reckoned a woman who could stand anything, had gone to live with relatives in Norfolk. She put the place up for sale, and when the Greyhound opened a month later under new management, the bar had been moved and the floorboards torn up to leave no trace of the event.

It happened that Waters was a known thief. Not a burglar exactly, but a man who kept his eyes and ears open, noting unlocked doors and unattended property and seizing such opportunities as presented themselves. All assumed he had come to grief whilst pursuing that occupation. Opinion varied on whether he had had some accident with machinery or whether a householder defending his property had assaulted him.

Exactly how the fatal blow had been dealt remained a mystery and a matter of speculation.

A folded page from an old book was found in Waters' pocket. Those who had seen it described a sort of pentagram drawn in black ink. The inquest did not mention that. Perhaps it savoured too much of cheap fiction, and they feared the newspapers would have made a sensation.

As for the cause of death, the coroner recorded only that a cutting implement had been employed on Waters' skull with fatal results. The coroner was a religious man and a lay preacher, and he said a good deal more off the record. When he told his audience he had seen the touch of the devils' hand with his own eyes, they were inclined to believe him.

Another point not in the papers, was that Waters' last utterances included not only the devil but also the name "Shackleton". Knowing that might have saved me from some of what followed.

ROUND ONE: THE ANTIQUE DEALER

A BELL TINKLED ABOVE THE shop door as I entered. Even though I had already removed my bowler, I stooped as I stepped inside. The doorway was not really so low, but the cluttered and shadowy interior gave an impression of smallness.

Hat in hand, I moved past stags' heads and mahogany bookcases, candelabras, and stuffed pheasants under glass domes. A gentleman writing in a sporting newspaper once described my appearance in the boxing ring as "pachydermous". That turned out to be his way of saying I reminded him of an elephant. Now I was an elephant in an antique shop, an animal more perilous than a bull in a china shop. I conducted myself accordingly, moving lightly and taking care not to disturb anything.

People compare many such shops to Aladdin's cave, but this one must have been an Aladdin of the poorest sort. Very ordinary lumber, odd furniture, and statuary for which the appellation of antique is an honorary one filled the shop. There were display cases of semi-precious stones and odd knick-knacks of ivory and painted china, the ugly and unfashionable items of a few decades ago that clutter England's antique shops. The well-arranged stock, I should say, made a good show. However, on my valuation—and mine is an informed one—the lot would not have fetched more than a hundred pounds. This was only Chichester and not London, but still I felt Mr Mellors' emporium was second-rate. The large fireplace, perhaps the best feature, threw out a very welcome heat. It was February, and a hard one. I paused a minute to warm my hands on the fire.

A dapper figure, a man in his middle years sporting a neat moustache, appeared in a doorway to one side. He was not at all the hearty character I was expecting. His green jacket, of a decidedly foreign cut, matched with a burgundy cravat. His expression indicated displeasure

"The wardrobe isn't going until tomorrow," he said.

"Excuse me. Perhaps there is a misunderstanding. I should like to speak to Mr Mellors, if that would be possible and convenient at this time."

"He speaks," he said with an arch little smile, dancing away behind an aisle formed by Japanese screens. "I thought you were here to collect a wardrobe."

I did not believe his deliverymen usually wore suits and ties, and wing collars. "If it would be possible to speak with Mr Mellors," I persisted. "At his convenience, I would be obliged."

China clattered as he rearranged something on a glass tabletop. "I don't know if it is convenient," he replied at last. "Not today."

I waited, and a minute later, his head reappeared around the screen.

"You'll only come back though, won't you?"

"I can return at a more convenient time, or in another place."

"May as well be now, I suppose," he said heavily. "What's it about?"

"Would you be Mr Mellors?"

"Would I be Mr Mellors? Look at Mellors Antiques." His sweeping gesture took in the whole shop. "Who would be Mr Mellors in their right mind, I ask you?"

I took this as an affirmative. "It's about your brother. The late Sir Ernest Shackleton."

"I know who my brother was, thank you very much."

"It's concerning a pecuniary matter. As you know, he left a number of debts, and I am exploring certain aspects of one on behalf of a legal firm."

"Are you now?" He relaxed slightly. "That's a new one. This might take more than a minute. Cup of tea, Mr...?"

"Stubbs," I supplied. "Of Latham and Rowe of Upper Norwood." As always, I felt a twinge of pride. Harry Stubbs, the butcher's boy, now the employee of a firm of solicitors. Harry Stubbs, who could barely read his name at school, entrusted with delicate legal matters.

"Upper Norwood," he said with a sigh. "I supposed the Palace is still a social whirl? Do sit down, Mr Stubbs. The kettle's just boiled."

I selected a seat with some care. Much of the furniture, of spindly, insubstantial manufacture, a type more suited to display than providing support. It does not do to sit on antiques, not ones that creaked when I settled on them. I lowered myself onto a solid chest that doubled as a bench. I could hear Mellors filling the teapot next door.

"Your brother left some rather significant debts and no ready means of repaying them."

Laughter brayed from the other room. "Dear old Ernest, the hero, the adventurer! He didn't have the slightest notion of money. Forty thousand pounds in debt, can you imagine it? How could you or I ever spend forty thousand, Mr Stubbs?"

"He organised a number of expeditions to the Antarctic. I believe that accounts for the bulk of the expenditure."

"He spent it indulging his whims, playing his big boys' games. If you or I did that, we'd be called criminals. Nobody ever charged *him* with fraud. My brother was a marvel."

"He intended to repay his debts." I extracted the notebook from my breast pocket and turned the crisp pages. "He communicated to various persons his full confidence of it."

7

"Pooh." Mellors emerged with two steaming cups on a tray, placing one of them on a delicate table by my elbow. "He may have said that, but you know we're Irish, and Ernest kissed the Blarney Stone when he was a baby." He broke into stage-Irish. "Sure and there'll be gold at the end of this rainbow, so there will, I've seen it myself, a whole crock of it, just spare me a thousand guineas for one more expedition... Do you think his backers believed there would be a financial return?" He pulled up a chair and resumed his usual voice. "Ernest made fools of everybody."

"I dare say you're right." I put the notebook aside and raised the dainty cup with some care, using my thumb and forefinger. The china was thin and translucent as eggshell. There was no milk, and the tea smelled strange and tasted stranger still.

"It's camomile," said Mellors.

It is in the nature of things that people treat you according to your appearance. If you look like a Duke, people will respect you. If you look like a nail, they will hammer you. As I look like a bear, so I expect them to bait me. "Very refreshing," I said.

"And what was it you wished to ask me?"

"It is a mystery indeed how anyone would expect to find money in the Antarctic." I paged through my notebook. "Sir Ernest was always interested in treasure, wasn't he? And he hinted to sundry people that he had brought something back, from, I believe, the Endurance expedition."

Mellors was listening, his head cocked slightly to one side.

"Now he only retuned from that expedition with what he was carrying on his person." I consulted my notes and the calculations I had made with the aid of a ready reckoner. "If we suppose that it was gold, which is priced at twenty pounds sterling per ounce Troy, then even three pounds of gold would be worth nine hundred and sixty pounds and ten shillings. It's a very considerable sum of money, but it doesn't approach the amount needed for his purposes." "I can tell you've made a thorough study of this, Mr Stubbs," said Mellors gravely.

"As a matter of fact, when the expedition made for home after the wreck of the *SY Endurance*, Sir Ernest made great play of throwing away gold sovereigns because they were too heavy to carry. So anything he brought back would have to be—if I may coin a phrase—worth more than its weight in gold. What sort of thing could that be?"

"What indeed?"

"Being as you are an expert in antiquities, and especially in gemstones and jewellery, I thought Sir Ernest might have consulted you on any valuables he might have acquired or hoped to acquire."

Mellors sipped his camomile tea as he considered that. "And that's your entire chain of reasoning?"

"Yes, sir. I might mention at this juncture that there would be remuneration if I were successful in recovering something of value. I am not at liberty to make promises, but a finder's fee of ten percent is quite usual in these matters. "

"You thought Ernest might have asked me to fence the stuff for him."

I had not expected to hear such a blunt expression from the criminal underworld. "I wasn't thinking in those terms at all. I just thought, being as he was your brother, he might have consulted your expertise."

"Well, I have to disappoint you, Mr Stubbs. My brother was not in the habit of trusting me—me, of all people!—with valuable information. Nor did he ever ask for my expertise, such as it is."

"That's a great pity. But can you tell me, are you aware of any valuable finds from the Antarctic region? Is there anything it's known for?"

"It's known for ice and snow, and penguins and whales. There are no people there."

I recalled *Nanook of the North*, that great cinematic epic of the Polar Regions, documenting the life of the Eskimo. I had seen it twice, and it made me shiver in the warmth of the Sydenham picture house to watch the doughty Nanook struggling against the polar blizzards and building his house out of ice blocks. "I believe I saw some carved penguins in one of your display cases?"

"Very astute, Mr Stubbs! My small tribute to Ernest... those are scrimshaw, carved by bored whalers. The best specimen is narwhal horn and has provenance to 1824. But they're not priceless relics. Antarctica does not produce indigenous art. The oldest things there are the empty tin cans left by brother Ernest's mob of ruffians."

"He never mentioned anything that he found, or hoped to find, that might appear valuable?"

"He talked all the time," said Mellors. "Ernest always said he was going to go off and find Captain Kidd's treasure or something, but he never did. We grew up on the *Arabian Nights*, and I don't think he ever got over it."

Having delivered the final verdict on his brother, he put down his cup. I might have objected, but it struck me then how hard it might be to have an elder brother like Sir Ernest, and how that might colour his opinion.

"Well, thank you for the tea, Mr Mellors. If anything should occur to you, I do hope you'll write to me care of Latham and Rowe."

"Treasure hunting," he said. "When we were children, he'd get our sisters and me into parties to go and dig up the garden for pirates' gold. He'd always tell us he had a map, and we always believed him. Underneath the fourth plank from the right-hand wall in the summerhouse... now he's got you chasing it, and he's not even alive! Dear old Ernest."

"Mr Rowe is convinced of the possibility of something of value."

Mellors snorted. "Value? There's a chap called Harcourt who wants to assemble a private museum. He pays well for anything 'Shackletonian'. If you've got an old sledge or an armchair of Ernest's, he might give you five pounds for it. I sold him a few souvenirs. You might try the same."

That suggestion was evidently facetious, and I did not record it.

"Are you a boxer, Mr Stubbs?" Mellors asked suddenly.

My physiognomy betrays the marks of the ring; I have the ears and nose of a boxer. "As a matter of fact, I was. I boxed for the Royal Regiment of Artillery in the war and afterwards on the circuit for a couple of years."

"I knew it from the way you moved when you came in. On your toes. I knew you had to be a boxer or a dancer. I've spent some time in boxing gymnasiums. How do you come to be working for a lawyer?"

I explained briefly how my work collecting debts had brought me into contact with Latham and Rowe, who had offered me part-time occupation in serving processes and assisting with the recovery of monies from businesses. Tasks like the more cerebral current assignment had increasingly supplemented that, and I was now a full-time employee. They had even suggested that, with appropriate study, in time I might become an articled clerk.

My older brother worked in father's shop. He had married unexpectedly early and already had a family. It was not certain that the business could support me as well, so everyone was pleased that I had found an opening that was not at a rival butcher's.

"So they didn't send you here to duff me up! A great relief to both of us, I'm sure." Mellors chuckled as he spoke. I could not hold it against him. "Funny how we start out on one course and end up on another."

I must have looked perplexed at this, because he laughed aloud. "Evidently you don't know my history. I thought the whole world knew… I'm not sure whether to be flattered or insulted. If you represent the law, well, I am a criminal, a convicted fraudster—accused, tried, sentenced, and duly punished." He struck a dramatic pose as though handcuffed and smiled at my discomfort.

Of course, I knew he must have changed his name from Shackleton to Mellors for some reason but had not guessed it was anything so serious. "I'm sorry to hear it, sir."

"It's water under the bridge. I still get pestered with a few feeble attempts at blackmail or harassment. These days I live very quietly, though 'the sword outlives the scabbard' and all that. I assumed you were here on my account rather than dear Ernest's."

"Oh, no. And if you should think of anything in connection with your brother's legacy, I'd be very pleased to hear from you."

He seemed about to say something but closed his mouth and held out his hand. "You're chasing wild geese if you expect money out of Ernest," was all he said. "Goodbye, Mr Stubbs." He shook hands limply. I had expected a robust, booming sort of man like his explorer elder brother. I would say Mellors was more the aesthetic type.

I procured a stock of ham sandwiches from the station refreshment room to sustain me on the journey back to Victoria. On the way back, I confess I read *Kim* rather than any law books. I tried to ignore a man in the compartment with a bushy beard who kept stealing glances at me. I do not believe the spectacle of eating ham sandwiches is such a remarkable thing. Considering that my observer wore a beard like a privet hedge, which might itself be the object of some remark, I thought he could have had better manners.

I reflected that the crock of gold to which Mellors had referred seemed as elusive as ever—if not actually imaginary, as he clearly believed. It was not my place to question the instructions of my superiors. If they wished to send me in pursuit of wild geese, off I went. Perhaps they might find something useful in my report, in which I attempted to transcribe the whole conversation. It seemed to be all hints and suggestions but nothing solid. Nothing I could get to grips with. I just made the notes; better brains than mine could solve the mystery.

I spent an hour at the gymnasium that evening, mainly working out on the heavy bag. Some boxers make the mistake of taking a breather every thirty seconds, but you need to practice as you fight, with a continuous rhythm of punches for three minutes at a stretch. It's a good exercise, and one that helps make up for the physical inactivity of life as a pen pusher. It is a relaxation too, mixing with men whose minds are of a more down-to-earth cast. By the time we had watched some young lads sparring and discussed Jack Dempsey's latest bout, I was feeling myself again.

ROUND TWO: THE NATURALIST

AGAIN, THEY PUT ME TO asking what Shackleton brought back from the desolate polar wasteland, so valuable it was worth dying for. *What mysteries did his expedition encounter, of which they never spoke a word?*

Sir Ernest Shackleton is remembered as our second greatest polar explorer. Most put him a rung below Robert Falcon Scott, "Scott of the Antarctic" as the newspapers always call him, although the title is not genuine at all. It is simply a made-up epithet, no more official than Harry 'the Norwood Titan' Stubbs. I don't rate Scott so high; Shackleton will always be the greater of the two.

Neither man achieved the South Pole, but Shackleton made it to within a hundred miles on the *Nimrod* Expedition before deciding to turn back. That was the difference between them: Scott's men perished because he decided to go on—and they failed to reach the pole anyway—but Shackleton nobly put the lives of his men first. He turned back rather than continuing to his goal. Some thought it would have been better if he had planted the Union Jack at the Pole in 1909 and died there. He could have been a martyr to the Empire, as Scott later martyred himself. But Shackleton brought his men back alive, every one of them, from that expedition. Even more remarkably, he did the same with the *Endurance* expedition that followed it.

Shackleton had a genius for coping with disaster. When ice trapped the *Endurance*, he knew he would have to maintain morale in the icebound ship for several months until the spring melt. Months later, when the ice groaned, squeezed, and crushed the vessel, he abandoned ship and led his men, dragging two lifeboats, on an heroic trek across the ice. After months of travel and many adventures, they made it to the sea and left the ice at last, taking to the boats. Six days later, they finally made Elephant Island, where they hoped whalers would pick them up.

Shackleton then understood that their supplies would not last until the whaling season. With a handful of men, he undertook the eight-hundred-mile journey to South Georgia with rudimentary navigation tools in open boats. After sixteen gruelling days, dehydrated and exhausted, Shackleton finally made landfall. Then he discovered they were on the wrong side, and winds prevented them from sailing round the island to the whaling station. Shackleton faced his greatest trial, crossing the snow-clad mountains of South Georgia with no equipment.

Still he showed endless resource. When finally they arrived at a peak above their objective, Shackleton fashioned a toboggan from a coils of rope and they flew down the last two miles. I should have been no more astonished if he had woven a magic carpet.

With every setback, he picked himself up and set a new goal. And he did not stop until he steered a Chilean ship to Elephant Island and rescued every single one of his men.

It's not just because Shackleton came from Norwood, like me, or because he had humble origins, like me, that I rate him greater than Scott. No, it's because he gave up glory in the name of humanity. That is the stuff of greatness. I would have followed him anywhere, if he'd have had me.

Any other man might have hung up his boots after *Endurance*, a great enough adventure for any three lifetimes. But not Sir Ernest. Like Sinbad the sailor, he kept going back for another adventure. Settled life never satisfied him.

Sir Ernest was a British hero, and it is not for the likes of me to pass comment on his heroism. However, I do feel able to say a word about Mr Shackleton the private man, speaking as one who takes a professional interest in such matters. His management of domestic economy was shocking. His wife and children survived on a pittance, supplied by her own private means.

Not so much credit as pure optimism funded his expeditions, and he started arranging one before he had even paid off the debts for the last. He spent money he did not have in the expectation that somebody would foot the bill afterwards.

In my line of work, I often meet dreamers. They are men of great conviction and, more often than not, very great talkers. These are, without exception, men with large debts and no way of paying them. They always want to explain why you should not bother about money but follow your dream.

I am not so much a dreamer. I am sent to collect money.

In the boxing game, a man who harbours illusions will get them knocked out of him. No, I don't seek to look very far beyond the facts and the hard reality of coins and folding stuff. Give us this day our daily bread, and the rest can look after itself.

Shackleton was a dreamer, and he left forty thousand pounds of debt when he died. Debt, promises of payment, and the notion of a great treasure that would pay for the lot. He dropped many hints to people around him. Most people, like Frank Mellors, assume these were empty promises of El Dorado. But some, my employers among them, detected a germ of truth in his tales. And that was why I found myself on the outskirts of Croydon, clutching a parcel wrapped in brown paper and looking for the house of a certain Dr Evans.

I did not wish to presume by arriving early, and my watch was not exact to the minute. Too cold to wait around, I walked up and down until a church's chimes struck the hour. As I turned around to go back to the house, a man scuttled away at the end of the street, and it seemed to me that he must have been following me. Now he was gone. I checked up and down the road before knocking at the door, firmly but politely.

I had written requesting an interview, and Dr Evans had invited me to visit at my convenience. I knew as little of Evans as I did of Mellors—even less, as it turned out. A man with grey hair, dressed casually in a waistcoat and an open-necked shirt, opened the door. He was smiling even before he opened it and seemed amused that he had to look up at me. He adjusted his gaze and craned his neck in an exaggerated fashion.

"Would you be Dr Evans?" I asked.

"No indeed, I wouldn't," he said, in the lilting singsong of a Welshman. "But I think she's expecting you. Come in, come in."

This was Mr Evans. The Dr Evans I was looking for was his wife. Like him, she was in her sixties. Her untidy grey hair was done up in a bun, with many strays wisps escaping. I did not have the impression that she troubled excessively over personal appearance. But she was a lively individual, and she showed me into a little parlour as neat as anything I could have wished for, with a fine oak dresser and plates displayed on the wall—good quality hand-painted china imported from Wales, I judged.

Watercolours depicting coastal scenery adorned the walls, and there was a framed embroidery in a foreign language above the fireplace. It felt I had stepped out of London into another country.

The only slightly disagreeable aspect was a pervasive smell of damp earth.

Mr Evans insisted that I have some tea and perhaps something to eat. I attempted to decline—rumour said that Welshmen eat seaweed for a delicacy and I did not wish to give offence —but his great persistence compelled me to accept. The maid was exiled to the scullery while Mr Evans bustled about in the kitchen. His wife sat down to talk with me like a man: no small talk but straight to business.

"This is the item I mentioned in my correspondence." I produced the parcel.

Dr Evans unwrapped it and extracted the battered volume with a smile of recognition.

"Your name is written inside the cover," I said. "I believe you loaned this book to Sir Ernest Shackleton, Dr Evans. I am pleased to be able to return it to you."

"It's Lucetti," she said. "I had been wondering what had happened to him. Yes, I suppose I did lend it to that explorer—Shackleton?"

"Sir Ernest Shackleton," I supplied. "The noted Antarctic explorer. Now deceased."

"He died, did he? There's a pity; he was such a nice man. And it's so nice talking to someone who takes a real interest."

"I would never ask you to break a confidence, Dr Evans, but it might be useful to my investigation if you could tell me something of the substance of what passed between you."

At that point, the return of Mr Evans with a tray bearing all the necessaries of teatime, which he distributed about with great skill, interrupted us. The tea was like English tea, and the tea cakes were excellent. Afterwards he sat down to a book with a title in a language I could not read.

I was explaining Shackleton's financial embarrassment and the possibility of a reward, but Dr Evans was reminiscing. "He was a gentleman, that Shackleton," she said. "So polite and very jolly, he was. And he was interested in my work with the tardigrades, as you can imagine."

I paused in my note taking. "Your work with what?"

"Tardigrades," she said clearly. "That's my field of study, tardigrades. Some people say I'm a bit of an authority when it comes to tardigrades, though I wouldn't make any claims for myself. All I know is how much I don't know. They're stranger than you can imagine."

"T-a-r-d-i-g-r-a-d-e-s." I spelled the word as it sounded.

"Slow walkers. Moss piglets. Water bears. The most indestructible creatures on the planet, found in every corner of earth. Unchanged for hundreds of millions of years." She reached past me for a book and opened it to a drawing showing a peculiar creature like nothing I had ever seen. It had six legs, and peculiar tendrils sprouted from its head. It looked like something from a fairy-tale, but the book was a perfectly respectable scientific textbook with a Latin name on the drawing.

"They are found on every corner of the planet. Would that include Antarctica?"

"Well yes, of course."

"I wasn't aware there were animals other than penguins there. Isn't it rather inhospitable?"

"Nothing is too inhospitable for tardigrades." Evans laughed. "They thrive on it! Heat, cold, even the vacuum of interplanetary space, they can survive anywhere." She raised her eyebrows. "Perhaps they even came from space. We don't know enough about their taxonomy to say just yet. Fascinating, they are."

Interplanetary space, I noted and added a question mark of my own.

"The thing about tardigrades, you see, is that they can suspend their animation. They need water, but when there's none, they just shut themselves down. If there's no food, or it's too dry or too cold, they withdraw their limbs into a barrel-shaped form with a tough outer layer, called a tun. Their body chemistry changes in all sorts of ways we can't begin to understand, depending on the conditions. And they stay like that until conditions improve. I thought Sir Ernest might bring me back some Antarctic tardigrades. They're very rare."

"And valuable?" I asked hopefully.

"No! Who'd pay money for a tardigrade? Shackleton was interested in suspended animation, and I can see why."

"Why would that be?"

She stopped, as though the question of why anyone would be interested had never occurred to her. "I imagine it would be for these expeditions, do you see? The men can't move in winter and they just stay there, cooped up, eating food and using fuel—and going potty from the cold and the dark, look you. But if they could go into suspended animation, they could just sleep through the winter and wake up in spring." Evans beamed at me, full of enthusiasm. "And the same for the long sea voyages. You could pack passengers in the hold like sacks of coal."

"It's a remarkable proposition," I said. "Science uncovers new wonders every day."

"Unfortunately nobody knows how tardigrades do it, so we can't copy the trick. Not yet, anyhow. But I am pursuing, as you might say, some lines of enquiry. Would you like to see a tardigrade? I have a laboratory of sorts next door."

"You mean to say you have one in the house? Are they dangerous?"

"No indeed, Mr Stubbs, they're not dangerous. Let me show you."

After exchanging a few words in a foreign language with her husband, she led me to the garden and into a spacious wooden structure. The interior looked more like a potting shed than a scientific laboratory. I could see no pens or cages, but all became clear when Evans adjusted some apparatus and gestured for me to take a look. It was a scientific microscope.

I had never used a microscope before. It took a minute for me to get the trick; the illuminated circle danced away from me until I found how to look through properly. But when I stood perfectly still, my jaw fell as I saw it. A creature with a clumsy, segmented body was pushing its way through tiny green fronds. It undulated in a most odd fashion. This creature was even more striking than the one in the drawing. It raised its head and seemed to look up at me for a second before carrying on.

"*Echiniscus*," said Evans. "Collected from my own garden. Shake out any piece of moss anywhere in the world, and you'll always you'll always find a few tardigrades."

"How big...?"

"One sixteenth of an inch for an adult specimen. But it depends on the species. Some are bigger than others."

Perhaps only size makes a monster. The tardigrade had something of the mythical beast about it but shrunk to such a scale it was curious rather than horrible. Perhaps if I were a foot shorter, people would not look at me so.

"It's gone," I said. The creature had meandered out of view.

Evans shoved me out of the away—something most men hesitate to do—and adjusted the slide. Once more, I watched the little beast pushing through its miniature jungle. It might have been a monster in the rain forests of tropical Venus.

"I have never seen anything like it in my life," I said. "I'm very grateful to you for the opportunity. What is it the poet says about there being more things in heaven and earth than we dream of?"

"Yes indeed," said Dr Evans, beaming. "And the more you look at tardigrades, the more you see."

"But as for the reason for Sir Ernest's interest..."

She paused, one hand on the microscope. "Well, we did talk up and down about suspended animation and how long it might last for. He asked me if a tardigrade might be revived after thousands of years in the ice."

"Thousands of years?"

She held up her hands. "And of course we don't really know; we haven't been experimenting long enough. But who knows? I wouldn't like to say it was impossible myself. That would be something, a living being older than an oak tree, older than the pyramids, pre-dating all human history. "

I wrinkled my forehead as I wrote down her words. An ancient tardigrade would be a wonder of the scientific world, to be sure, but I doubted somehow that it carried any great value. It wasn't the sort of thing one could exhibit in a travelling menagerie unless substantially larger than the flea-sized creature I had witnessed.

"I recall now," she said. "He did ask a most unusual question. He asked me how tardigrades communicated."

"And how do they communicate?"

"It's a very good question, but I'm afraid science isn't ready for it yet." She held her finger and thumb about an inch apart. "This is how much we know about tardigrades." She spread her arms wide to measure out a fathom. "And this is what we don't know about them. But as I said to your Mr Shackleton, I'm working on it."

I thanked Dr Evans fulsomely for her time. She seemed pleased that she had found another student. My head was buzzing with strange monsters, and animation suspended for thousands of years, and ships full of frozen passengers. I returned to the office to write up my report for Mr Rowe.

I did not feel entirely at ease in the office. It was not just that the narrow doorways and cramped spaces were uncomfortable for my size; it was the atmosphere of the place. Solicitors' offices are, I suppose, intimidating to anyone not born to the business. I couldn't help feeling out of place; the brisk young clerks and the indifferent older clerks generally did not have much to say to me. The secretaries were polite, and the errand boys were talkative but sometimes cheeky—I sometimes got calls of "A pound of minced beef and four pork chops!" when I walked in. To the partners themselves, I was of course invisible.

The one unfailingly pleasant person was Mrs Crawford, the Senior Secretary. She was a force to be reckoned with, the great clearinghouse for all communications between the office staff and the solicitors themselves. She had two desks, one with a typewriter and one with a kind of wooden pigeonholing.

All feared Mrs Crawford. She was sometimes moved to state, in a voice audible in every corner, that she took no nonsense from anyone. Even the boldest of the clerks hesitated to interrupt her when she was engaged in paperwork. If she conveyed to a supplicant that she would most certainly not pass on any such request to Mr Rowe, she did it with such force that the request was never repeated.

Fortunately, Mrs Crawford was never less than cordial with me.

I took my desk, nodding a few greetings to my colleagues. Then I set about writing an account of my interview with Dr Evans while still fresh in my mind. I consulted a dictionary as needed and wrote a fair copy after I drafted the report. It is a slow but necessary process in the legal world; every five-minute conversation takes two hours to get onto paper. But a verbal report is just empty air that vanishes, whereas a paper report is a lasting thing.

When I had finished, Mrs Crawford took up the papers and glanced through them. My first reports had been clumsy affairs that I had to rewrite many times before I could submit them. I worked late to get them into shape. But after that difficult apprenticeship, I felt I had mastered the written form. I still felt a tinge of apprehension as Mrs Crawford looked through my work, though. Some of the others said she made them feel they were schoolboys in a class over which she was mistress, and there was a grain of truth in that.

"Very good, Mr Stubbs," she said politely, after paging through it.

"I hope Mr Rowe finds the information useful. Though I can't connect it to the rest of the matter myself."

"We'll leave that to Mr Rowe." She filed it away in one of her pigeonholes, though not the one labelled for Mr Rowe's immediate attention. "And this came for you."

The envelope was postmarked from Chichester and opened, which was routine. The note inside contained just two lines and was neither signed nor dated.

Another man asked after the same thing as you two years ago. He died violently soon afterwards. Please be careful.

I surmised it came from Sir Ernest's brother, Frank Mellors. Although I did not have his usual hand to compare it with, the writing seemed unsteady. He may have written it hurriedly, or perhaps he was in some state of agitation. Perhaps Mr Rowe would understand the significance of those two lines and the nature of the threat implied, but to me it was obscure.

ROUND THREE: THE EXPLORER

THERE IS NOTHING LIKE A London pub for comfort. The Conquering Hero is my local, the warm fug, thick with tobacco and beer, the sawdust and oyster shells underfoot. This is where a man can relax, stretch his legs out, and drink in the company of other men. Where you can laugh as loud as you like, and swear, and spit, and not be looked at. You could sing round the piano and forget your cares. If there is a more comfortable place in all the world, then I haven't found it.

I could not quite believe that Henry Brown, late of the *Endurance* expedition, was really going to come here. It was as though I had issued an invitation to a character from a storybook. Mr Brown said he did not mind where we met, so long as it was convivial, and it seemed only natural to invite him to the Hero.

While I waited for him, I leafed through *South*, Sir Ernest's magnificent account of the *Endurance* expedition. What a tale it is! On one occasion, when the party was camped on an ice floe, Sir Ernest left his tent late at night, motivated by an almost psychic uneasiness. The ice cracked practically under his feet, in the middle of the tents. He saw a white object floating below and hauled out a sleeping bag with a man in it a second before the ice-edges came back together with tremendous force. The man, Holness, was unhurt, but he must have been frozen to the bone. There is no finer place to read those adventures than the cosy warmth of the public bar, with the February wind howling outside to remind one of the Antarctic gales.

Having studied the photographs from the expedition, I recognised Brown at once when he came in. He was a healthy, handsome man, if not overly clean-shaven. He was not one of the more notable members of the party, having been left on Elephant Island, but nevertheless he had participated in that glorious adventure. We shook hands heartily. Brown shrugged off his greatcoat and explained without embarrassment that he had walked all the way from Clapham Junction due to lack of ready funds. I immediately stood him a brandy to take the chill off, which he accepted gratefully. I ordered two pints of bitter at the same time.

Mr Rowe's tersely worded assignment instructed me only to interview Brown and ascertain anything relevant to the Shackleton legacy. I would have preferred more to go on. Like the explorers, I was heading out into trackless wastes, with no map to guide me but simply following a bearing.

I need not have worried that Brown would be taciturn. He was a gentleman but not one of the stuffy sort. He was more like the sporting gentlemen who talk avidly about the fancy to anyone without regard for social distinctions. Brown soon engrossed me in his story of the Antarctic expedition. I drank it in and tried to remember to ask questions and make notes when I could. There was a good buzz of conversation around us, and I had little concern about being overheard.

"He knew how to keep morale up and jolly us all along," mused Brown. "Always starting a round of songs or games, or story-telling. And poetry, too—he could quote reams of the stuff, mainly Browning. 'A man's reach should exceed his grasp' and that... he wouldn't put up with gloom."

"Did he ever talk about fossils?" I asked.

"Fossils? He wasn't much interested in that sort of science stuff."

"Not even if it meant important new discoveries?"

"That wasn't his idea of discovery! The Boss wanted lost cities and palaces piled high with treasures. King Solomon's Mines were more in his line. I suppose he might have been satisfied with a valley full of dinosaurs, if we could have brought a few of them back alive." Brown's mouth twitched into a smile. "As I recall, he tried to tell us there were giant pterodactyls nesting in the crater of Mount Erebus."

"He actually told you that?" I asked, bemused.

"I imagine they were just albatross, but you needed field glasses to tell. Oh yes, the Boss would spin six impossible stories before breakfast. He was a great one for tall tales and practical jokes. Ribbing us about penguins that talked like parrots, or saying to look out for ice goblins. You know he once came limping back from a seal hunt, covered in blood, saying he'd been mauled half to death by a sea elephant? Of course it was just seal blood he'd smeared all over himself, but he didn't half give us a fright."

"Wasn't it confusing, never knowing what you could believe?"

"It was part and parcel of his magic. With him, you always believed that the fantastic might just happen." He took a swig of beer. "Polar expeditions are always against the odds. A realist would give up before he started. But a man like the Boss... it's men like him who make it to impossible places, even when the others are saying it can't be done."

"But he was a practical man—"

Brown laughed and slapped the table. "He was never practical! His schemes never worked out, like those ridiculous motor sledges. He never mastered driving dogs or even skiing, or anything technical. He was brilliant at improvisation, though. Give him a piece of rope, a broken chisel, and a banjo, and he'd lead an expedition over the Himalayas. And the banjo would be the important thing. He jollied us all along with promises of the riches of Fata Morgana—"

"Of what?"

"Fata Morgana. A fairy city of spires and towers in the distance you see quite often down South. It's an optical illusion, caused by refraction off seawater or ice or something. It can make whole phantom mountain ranges. The Boss could tell you all about it. The Arabs call it the City of Genies, I remember that."

"'A beautiful dazzling city of cathedral domes, spires and minarets,'" I quoted, to show I knew what he was talking about. Only his pronunciation of the name Fata Morgana, which I had not heard spoken aloud before, had confused me. "But surely there can't be any cities there?"

"Who knows? The Boss said there was a genuine Fata Morgana, and that the mirages were projections of it—like seeing an oasis from dozens of miles away."

"The Antarctic seems like an unlikely place for a treasure hunt."

"The Boss didn't think so. He loved treasure hunts. He once hid his mother's jewellery in the garden shed and had the whole family looking for it… but as he said, thousands of people had been hunting for the hoard left by Alaric the Goth after he sacked Rome, and the Crown Jewels that King John lost in the Wash. But nobody else had ever searched the Antarctic before us."

"But there's nothing but ice and snow…"

"Now, maybe, but in ages past… you should have heard him on the subject! He was full of Celtic legends and ancient manuscripts. Ever hear of the Piri Reis map? A Turkish admiral pieced it together in the sixteenth century, from maps older than Noah. It shows the coastline of Antarctica, hundreds of years before Europeans set foot there, with trees and animals. The Boss said he'd studied it and there were some marks worth investigating."

"I don't think he ever mentioned anything like that in his book."

"He always knew the right story for the person he was talking to," said Brown. "And he charmed thousands of pounds out of the backers, when you or I couldn't get sixpence."

I went to the bar for two more pints. At the mention of money, I could not help but notice Brown's own condition. His shortage of funds was not temporary. His woollen sweater, like his greatcoat, was showing its age, and his shoes had been mended more than a few times. Nothing about him spoke of prosperity, and he drank his beer as though he had not tasted its nectar in year. Life was not simple for ex-explorers.

A man with a distinctive unkempt beard was drinking alone in the next booth. I did not know him, but I had seen him before. *Is he listening to us?*

"Even if you reached your Fata Morgana," I said, placing a mug in front of Brown, "even if it had tombs as rich as Tutankhamen's, and they were intact, and you managed to break into one... you wouldn't be able to carry out much on a sled." I could not recall my exact calculations on the amount of gold an Antarctic explorer could carry, but they were in my notebook. "And as soon as the place was known, you couldn't stop others from coming afterward and there being a free-for-all."

"That was one of the Boss's favourite riddles. Suppose we did reach Fata Morgana itself, and we found the treasure room in the royal palace—piles and piles of loot, —and you could only take out what you could carry. What would you have? He had us talking about that for days."

I scratched my chin. This sort of exercise requires a special type of imagination. Sir Ernest had it to excess, but I am perhaps deficient. I tried to see myself in some treasure room, like the colour plate in the *Arabian Nights* book I read as a boy. "I supposed I'd fill my pockets with gems and jewels."

"But how would you know if they were real ones or paste?" Brown smiled. "That's what the Boss always said. How would you know if they were stones that were valuable to the ancients but worthless these days, like quartz or coloured glass?"

I have some skill in valuation, but jewellery is a specialist's job. I rubbed my chin thoughtfully, not wishing to appear foolish.

"If it's a necklace with stones as big as grapes then it's bound to be costume stuff," Brown went on. "Ever seen the Crown Jewels in the Tower? They're not half as impressive as the stones the girls wear in Shaftesbury Avenue shows. How do you tell?"

"Well, I don't know much about gemstones. What's the answer?"

"Oh, you don't get out of it that easy." He laughed, enjoying the game. "The Boss would string us out with this sort of thing for hours, days. What about works of art, eh? What about priceless books? Portable wealth... we'd spend whole evenings arguing about it, and about what we'd spend the money on afterwards. The Boss knew how to keep us going. It's funny, but even though you know the whole thing is one of his fantasies, you do get to thinking."

"Thinking what?"

Brown was looking at the wall, but I imagined he was seeing a perfectly white landscape stretching endless out under a blue sky. Just him and two dozen others, the only humans for a hundred miles. Looking at the ice ridges and dunes and the deep crevasses that led down to the ancient bedrock far below. "Thinking if maybe there wasn't just some possibility you would find a lost city there. That maybe the Boss did know something about it, and maybe some of the others on earlier expeditions. Perhaps not every Fata Morgana was an optical illusion after all..." He looked up suddenly. "Crazy dreams, when you say them out loud in a place like this. But it's surprising what keeps you going in places like that."

"I can't imagine what it was like."

"Fresh fruit, that was an obsession of mine. I kept thinking we might find a greenhouse with oranges and pineapples and bananas growing in it—you know, there were days when that would have been more valuable to me than all the gold in the world, just to taste fresh fruit again. Sometimes the sunlight would catch sheet ice that had been swept clean by the wind, and the Boss would say ' look there, I think it might be one of Brown's greenhouses up ahead!'" He laughed and shook his head. "He was always the first to spot anything."

I did not see how it could be a happy memory, how he could look back with nostalgia to the bitter cold, the deprivation, the constant exhaustion, all the pains and sufferings of an Antarctic expedition. But he smiled as fondly as though it has been a week at the seaside.

A vendor was doing the rounds with a tray of jellied eels, and I bought two pots. Brown fell on his and devoured it with such gusto that I ordered a couple of savoury pies from a second vendor to go with them. As Brown ate, I looked through my notebook, scavenging for some scrap I could try him on. "There's a puzzling remark of Sir Ernest's here," I said. "About how 'future explorers will doubtless carry pocket wireless telephones fitted with wireless telescopes' and be fed by radio waves. What does it mean?"

"Another of the Boss's fancies." Brown shrugged. "He said we would be the last generation that could explore before the aeroplanes and airships covered the globe."

"Do you know what he was doing when he died?"

"It was his great final expedition, his swan-song. He wanted to go back south one last time."

"For what purpose?"

"Coastal mapping, looking for lost islands. That was the official reason. He wasn't aiming for the Pole, I know that. He said he never had any interest in it."

"Might he have been returning to a treasure hoard?"

"Who knows?" Brown shook his head and smiled. "With the Boss, who knows? He always said he'd die at forty-eight; a Gipsy told him once. I thought it was another of his stories, but his heart gave out just like that." His gaze fell on the clock above the bar. "Good Lord, is that the time? I'd better shoot off."

As we shook hands, Brown leaned closer and looked me in the eye. "Look here, Stubbs. You're a decent chap and all that. You know a fellow can't betray a confidence. If you do find anything—and I don't say there's anything to be found—just you remember what they say about sleeping dogs."

"What do you—"

Brown turned on his heel and was off, whistling into the night on the long walk to catch his train. He left me to order another pint and jot down notes on our conversation. I could tell his warning was deadly serious, but the meaning was opaque.

I could still feel his hand, the hand that had shaken Sir Ernest's, in mine. Indeed, the hand that might have embraced Sir Ernest, for the men slept in each others' arms to keep off the worst of the cold. Imagine that.

Brown was poor in material things but rich in spirit. I did not doubt he would find a place on an expedition up the Amazon or some such soon enough. His appetite for life was undimmed. Not like that wretch Armydale, who killed himself in Australia. Armydale had been a rich man with a wife and children. For some reason, he found life unbearable after he returned from the expedition. One evening he went to his club, put on his dress uniform, and shot himself.

There was no sign of the man with the bushy beard, but I observed a group of strangers in one booth. Their accents betrayed them as Irish labourers, not unusual. One finds groups of them everywhere, staying in the area for a few days or a few weeks, digging holes or working on construction sites. Some English folk take against them, but we don't have much trouble around these parts.

When I got up to leave, the Irish were smart about following suit. By the time I had wished goodnight to the barmaid and a few other acquaintances, they were already out the door.

Thirty yards from the pub, the pavement turns and widens, and there are iron railings on one side. The four Irish were waiting for me there, ranged across the pavement. They had adopted combative stances, and there was no mistaking their intention. The night air was very cold, and they exhaled plumes of steam like racehorses ready for the off.

"Mr Harry Stubbs," said one, the Irish brogue loud and clear. "We'd be wanting a word with you."

I looked along the row. One young fellow was almost my size, but the others were not in the same weight class. Clothes made the judgement difficult, but I placed the big fellow as a good heavyweight at sixteen stone, one a light heavyweight of about twelve stone, a welterweight of eleven stone, and another who might have been a lightweight. Obviously, size and weight are not the only considerations. Plenty of boxers have beaten men in a heavier class than their own, but for a trained fighter, weight counts for a good deal. I am about as big a size as heavyweights run to without being ungainly. I rolled my shoulders and flexed my arms.

"Will you look at the size of the fooker," muttered the welterweight.

I was in high good humour. A gallon of decent English bitter was singing through my veins. I would never back away from a fight. I removed my bowler and hung it on the iron railings next to me as though on a hat rack. "Gentlemen," I declared, unbuttoning my coat. "I am a working man myself. And I do believe you have taken money to do a job tonight." I hung the coat by my hat and unbuttoned my stiff collar. They were hanging back, a picture of irresolution. The air felt fresh and clean. "Well then," I said. "Let us go to our work."

You may say that I should have called for help or run back—the pub was just a few steps away, and if I had run, they could not have caught me before I got to the door. But I was feeling very well indeed. What lawyer's clerk does not feel a surge of excitement when he can finally break free from pen pushing? Who does not long to meet a problem he can solve by punching it?

"Only fools and dogs fight for no money," Sergeant Eagleton, my Army trainer, once told me. But there's no sense in having two good fists if you never use them.

At a nod from one of the others, the heavyweight moved forward alone. He was fully as confident as I was. He was a big, raw-boned sort who could not have been more than nineteen. His stance was untutored. He reminded me of myself at the same age: a boy who had been in a few fights and never lost one. We sparred for a few seconds, finding our measure.

"Go on Mickey," shouted one of the others. "Belt him one."

The boy let loose a right, but I backed away from it. He stepped closer and fired another right, which I blocked. That surprised him all right, and so did the left I planted in his midsection.

Mickey tried to get closer, and I backed up against the railings. One of the others was trying to circle around me, but I could not look around.

"Give him the haymaker!"

Mickey was a one-punch fighter, his well-developed blows much too obvious.

"You might as well send him a bleeding telegram and let him know a punch was coming," Sergeant Eagleton used to tell me.

He thrashed out energetically, but not skilfully enough to touch me. A truly skilled boxer can dodge every punch thrown by an amateur just by moving his head. I'm not so flash myself, but I can move. When Jack Dempsey answered a reporter that the man whose footwork he most admired was the ballet dancer Nijinsky, people took it as a joke.

After six blows in a row failed to connect, Mickey started to slow, and I responded with a series of quick left jabs. The jab is a short, direct blow, with nothing from the shoulder. It gives no warning. I doubt Mickey ever saw the punches that cut his face. He swung back, hitting only air. Bare-knuckle is by no means the same scientific exercise as a bout, according to the Marquis of Queensbury. But I showed that boy a few things I had been taught in the same hard way about the Noble Art.

Mickey's final attempt to land the solid punch that had felled every other opponent left him off-balance, his guard too low. I unleashed a full-blooded right-hander that put him out on the pavement. My knuckles would hurt next morning, but I did not mind.

The light heavyweight, who might have been his older brother, stepped up and swung a length of wood at me. I blocked with my left, and backed away. He swished again well wide then aimed a blow downward at my head. I stepped inside the swing and punched him in the solar plexus with my left. A boxer tenses his muscles so such blows have little effect, but the blow took the wind out of him. Then I gave him right and left uppercuts faster than you could count one-two, and he was on the ground with blood streaming from his nose.

"Get him," ordered the lightweight.

"Pogue mahone," the fourth man said. It's a rather crude Irish expression. With evident reluctance, he stepped into range and made unconvincing feints.

I moved back and forth a little, adjusting the distance for a knockout blow, but the fourth man came up on my other side, streetlight gleaming off a long steel blade. It affected me like a bucket of cold water.

It is a well-understood principle that the inferior party may pick up and use improvised weapons as convenient. A billiard cue, a bar stool, or similar blunt instrument, these are fair play when a party is sorely pressed. But never knives or other deadly weapons,

He crouched in a knife-fighters stance, ready to dart in while the other man threw shadow punches from too far off. If I tried to hit him, I'd get a knife in my guts from his comrade. I reached behind me and picked up my coat off the railing. Perhaps the knifeman expected me to whirl the coat and wrap it around my hand as a shield, as I have seen done in the pictures. Instead, I threw it at his face. The knifeman batted my coat aside, but it obstructed his vision enough for me to step in and stun him with a long left. A moment later, I had his wrist in my right hand.

The fourth man moved in, theatrically cocking his arm back for a blow; I jabbed his chin and he reeled backwards. I was minded to break the knifeman's arm for attempting to stab me, but young Mickey was getting to his feet. I flung the knifeman into the iron railings full force; he bounced off, and went down.

Mickey shook his head like a dog; as soon as he raised his guard, I knocked him down again with a clean right. The fourth man, made to run away but too slowly. I had him by the coattails and then by the collar. I took a fistful of his coat in my other hand and, lifting him bodily off the ground, heaved him back and threw him headlong into the gutter. He pulled himself up and scampered off down the road.

Harry Stubbs had proven himself champion again—and I had an audience, a dozen men who had spilled out of the pub.

"You all right, Harry?" asked someone.

"Never better," I said. "They didn't lay a glove on me."

Of course, nobody called the police, and that was the end of it. If I had my wits about me, I would have got the crowd to lay hold of my assailants. We could have twisted the arm of one of them until he told me what the thing was all about. Or I should have gone through the knifeman's pockets and seen if anything could have identified him. He was the ringleader, though I hadn't really appreciated it at the time.

But instead I drank a restorative brandy on the house and then another from a well-wisher, and listened to the story of the fight told and re-told. Jokes about my being the Conquering Hero were repeated endlessly. Afterwards

I had to let myself in with a latchkey and tiptoe quietly to bed, but all in all, it was a most satisfactory evening.

ROUND FOUR: THE CONSIGNMENT MAN

THE ELECTRIC WAS NO LONGER the only establishment on the street to boast electric lighting, but it retained the name nonetheless. It was the favourite breakfasting spot for those whose domestic circumstances could supply satisfactory catering, and it also served as a kind of informal club or meeting place. Many of its clientele carried their work out by night, and a hearty breakfast was the last meal of the day rather than the first. It was not a fancy eating-place, just an ordinary café; I dare say some would call it rough. But it had a comfortable, perhaps clannish, atmosphere for those of us who frequented it.

As I anticipated, Arthur Renville was hard at work on a plate of bacon, sausages, kidney, fried eggs, tomato, mushroom, and the usual accompaniments. The Electric always served Stubbs' Famous Pork & Beef sausages.

Arthur insisted on them, and Mario, the proprietor, knew better than to disappoint Arthur Renville.

"Wotcher, Stubbsy," Arthur called, gesturing for me to join him.

I had known Arthur most of my life. He did business with my father and was a kind of mentor for me. I was privileged to call him by his first name. On Arthur's advice, I left boxing after my second defeat. He told me that in the boxing game if you're not on the way up, you're on the way down, and I had best find other occupation. I was not easily convinced, but he was of course right. With his assistance, I found a place collecting debts.

Arthur had the look of a prosperous bookmaker. He was a wealthy man but not flash. He knew his place, though he had a certain air of command, and snapped his fingers for Mario.

"Cup of tea and the card for Mr Stubbs here."

"Morning, Arthur," I said. "I trust you and your family are in good health."

"Very much so, and my felicitations to your family also. But Stubbsy, I heard about this here affray outside the Conquering Hero last night. I want to assure you that it was entirely and completely outside my knowledge and without my cognisance. So help me God."

"I do believe and trust that to be the case, Arthur. It would never be my assumption otherwise."

"Well, I'm most gratified to hear it. To be frank with you, Stubbsy, it's disturbing to me that such an occurrence has occurred where it did."

Arthur was what is known in some circles as a Consignment Man. Most of them were East Enders from round the docks, but there were some south of the river, too. His type did not deal in individual items or small quantities but in entire consignments of goods whose provenance was questionable. If a load of pineapples rotted in transit, if Chinaware smashed on a rough voyage or salt water spoiled biscuits, then the owners went through the appropriate channels with Lloyds of London to recover their losses. And as often as not, a consignment of goods of similar description appeared on the market soon afterwards.

The consignment man was a master of logistics; he had drivers and vehicles at his beck and call; he knew of unused sheds and stables and a hundred other spaces where goods could be stored at short notice. He was on intimate terms with every criminal in the area. He knew a hundred businessmen and a thousand middlemen with an eye for good quality merchandise and cash down to pay for it.

As a boy, I heard rumours that Arthur dealt in stolen goods. He soon put me right on that one. Stolen property was too hot for him to handle, and he turned it down on principle. The consignments that found their way to him had always been properly written off and recorded as such.

"Then isn't it stolen from the owners?"

"Not at all. They're happy to see it gone. You see, the insurance value is always greater than the actual value of the consignment. The paperwork is always In Order, and Lloyds of London pays out on every one."

"So Lloyds are the ones losing out?"

Arthur laughed merrily at that. "Lloyds lose out! Stubbsy, you are too good for this wicked world. They don't lose a penny. The way it works is this: Jolly Jack Tar gets a bottle of grog, his Captain Courageous gets a new coat, the ship-owners get a fat cheque, and the gentlemen of Lloyds, why, they all take winter cruises in the Caribbean. And your esteemed father, Stubbs the Butcher, he gets his supplies cheap so he can make sausages with twice the meat at half the price of the competition. My merry men make themselves a few bob on the side and me, I dine in stately splendour at the Electric Rooms every morning."

"So where does the money come from?"

He tapped his nose confidentially. "The Good Lord provides, Stubbsy."

The Good Lord especially helps those who keep their wits about them. The proverbial sparrow does not fall in Norwood but that Arthur knows how much meat there is on it and what its feathers would fetch. And he'll make sure nobody takes it.

Arthur had a Consignment Man's capacity to prevent shrinkage, pilferage, and other forms of larceny in transit. Vermin were his biggest problem, he said. A consignment up halfway to perishing was a magnet for every mouse, rat, and other rodent for miles, and Arthur always kept a good supply of mousetraps on hand. And deterrents for the larger form of vermin, too.

He was not a harsh man. Arthur's rule was that there was plenty for everybody and everybody got his fair share. The only thing that spoiled it was if certain individuals became greedy. The consignment man ensured diligence all round and no sticky fingers. Otherwise, there were broken bones, slashed faces, and other ways of marking those who transgressed against the common weal of the consignment business.

Mario set down a blue china mug of tea and tried to pass me a stained menu, which I gravely declined. The tea was good, strong and sweet.

"As I heard it," said Arthur, "These five bog Irish jumped you as you was leaving the Hero. And you knocked seven bells out of them all. Serves them right."

"There were only four. And only one of them knew how to use his fists."

"But one of them had a knife?" Arthur shook his head at the villainy of it. He knew a thing or two about villainy, he could give lessons in it, but that was beyond the pale. His voice shook with emotion. "In the first place, that anyone should lay a finger on a personal friend of mine without the least prior consultation is a sore provocation to me. In the second place, that persons should be doing this kind of thing at all in this location is a thing not to be tolerated." He cut up his bacon and egg with unnecessary violence.

"I don't expect they'll be troubling me again, Arthur."

"I shouldn't be surprised if they did, though," he said darkly. "This was a put-up job, ordered, paid for, and delivered. They will most likely be back, if I know what's what, meaning to finish the job—ten of them, with iron bars in their hands. But I won't stand for it." He thrust a forkful of food into his mouth. After a minute, he continued in more measured tones. "Certain enquiries are being made in quarters where our Hibernian friends are likely to be known. As soon as these are completed, I will inform you toot sweet."

"That's very gentlemanly of you, Arthur."

He looked almost offended. "Least I can do, Stubbsy. I tell you, though, I wish I'd been there to see it. So what's this matter you're working on that gets this attention?"

A vow of confidentiality sealed Latham and Rowe, but Arthur Renville was an old friend and one whom I trusted implicitly. I told him about my attempts to track down anything of value that Sir Ernest Shackleton might have secreted. He laughed aloud when I told him about my interview with Mellors.

"I should think he did take exception. Old Frank Mellors! Didn't you read the papers about him stealing the Irish Crown Jewels back in '07? Before your time, I suppose."

"I didn't even know there were any Irish Crown Jewels."

"There aren't any more," Arthur chuckled. "Mellors and his cronies made off with them. Or at least, that's what everybody thinks. But it was all covered up." His voice dropped. "It seems they were all part of a… well… they say… a ring of homosexuals."

I had known odd individuals in boxing circles pointed out as "homosexual". But I had never heard that a man's approaches might be acceptable to another man, or that there were whole groups of them.

Arthur lowered his voice. "There was orgies, so they say. Men with men. With titled persons present and all."

"You're pulling my leg."

"That's why he changed his name and moved to England. He's on his uppers."

"No wonder he was offended when I was asking him about jewels." I wished I had known the story before the interview.

"Don't worry, Harry. It doesn't do to be too clever. And this Dr Evans woman—anything suspicious about her?"

"She would have kept talking about her tar-di-grades for as long as I cared to listen. But I'm blowed if I can see what they have to do with anything else."

"Did you think about gold? One gold nugget would be worth a king's ransom."

"But the weight of gold…"

"It is not the value of the sample; it's the vein of gold it points to. The Antarctic could be the next Klondike, except it's a sight harder to go prospecting there. It could be worth millions."

"I'll look into that. I did have one thought of my own. The other evening I was reading an account of Robert Falcon Scott's ill-fated expedition of 1912."

"I don't think anyone every actually says 'ill-fated', Stubbsy."

I paged through my notebook to the section I had copied out. "What caught my attention was what was found on Scott after he died. It seems he had been collecting some particular stones."

"What sort of stones?"

"That great explorer filled his pockets with fossils. Even though they had to shed as much weight as possible, those fossils were of the greatest value. Scott collected these fossils from the Beardmore Glacier the behest of a Dr Suess, who I understand to be an Austrian geologist. The reason being, these fossils prove the theory of continental drift, inasmuch as they are the remains of tropical plants. This proves that Antarctica once enjoyed a warm climate, a finding of not inconsiderable significance."

"Maybe so," said Arthur. "But how do you convert that into pounds, shillings, and pence? I never heard of a trade in them, not like artworks and gemstones. Fossils are more what you call curios. On the other hand, those four Irish weren't set on you for curios."

"I suppose not."

The bearded man who had been following me must have put them up to it. They thought either Brown had handed me something or had given me some information that made it worth attacking me. If only I knew what they thought I had.

Arthur must have been thinking along the same lines. "There's money in this," he said. "You keep your eyes peeled, Stubbsy, and mind what you're up to."

ROUND FIVE: THE SUMMERHOUSE

I WAS MOST CONCERNED ABOUT the possible repercussions when I submitted my report. I agonised about whether I should mention the brawl outside the Conquering Hero. In the end, I felt it must be relevant to the case. I feared Mr Rowe would be shocked that an employee should be engaging in a fracas, even cloaked in the terms with which I expressed it. Scuffles whilst collecting debts were common, but that was another case entirely.

I did have one straw to clutch at, and I took down some of the files relating to Shackleton. For the first time, the weight and volume of my own reports impressed me. I blushed to see the untidy early ones, all blots and crossings-out, and the workmanlike jobs I was now turning out satisfied me more.

I was looking for a gold mine. Shackleton did mention finding grains of gold on one mud sample, but the expedition geologist, Bibert Douglas, offered a more authoritative statement. He talked extensively with Shackleton on this exact topic and oversaw the analysis of the mineral samples, too. I doubt Shackleton could have put one over on him. Douglas was categorical about the lack of gold, silver, or other precious metals in any of their samples, however optimistic his superior had been.

I was on my way to replacing the files when Mr Rowe chanced to pass on his way out of the office. He was alone, so I decided to speak up. "Begging your pardon, Mr Rowe, sir," I began.

"Hmm, what is it?" He seemed surprised rather than annoyed that I had importuned him.

"I merely wished to reassure you, Mr Rowe, of my continuing fidelity to the firm." I fumbled for words. "I do hope that my recent report will not have created any bad impression, as I'm sure you will take the full circumstances into account."

"Ah well, yes, of course I will. I have realistic expectations. Was that all you wanted to ask?"

"Yes, sir."

"Very good. Well, well, keep up the good work, er, Stubbs." He nodded politely and continued on his way without a single word of reproach or even warning about my behaviour. That was better than I could have hoped. Afterwards, a new fear took me—perhaps he had not even read my report yet. But Mrs Crawford assured me he had read it and that he understood fully the unorthodox nature of the assignment and the nature of the incidents that consequently attended it.

"He thinks very highly of you," she said. "He told me he was quite satisfied with the progress of the Shackleton case." She passed me a thick manila envelope marked "private and confidential" and advised me not to read it until I was out of the office. Mr Rowe had used more precaution than usual to conceal my work from my colleagues, and on examining the contents, I discovered why.

Disputes and legal difficulties often hedge action to recover rightful property. If a thief steals your gold watch, are you permitted to burgle it back? Volumes and volumes of law books on the shelves at Latham and Rowe were devoted to this very topic, and it has provided ample employment for lawyers over generations.

In this instance, Mr Rowe assured me that stealth and subtlety would be the most expeditious approach, and that the old adage about possession being nine parts of the law was a valid one. That was not quite the first time I had accepted such a commission, but it was unusual. For such a mild-looking man, Mr Rowe had a surprising streak of the bandit about him; before I joined the firm, I had no idea that respectable solicitors employed such tactics. Truly, I was undergoing an education.

This assignment would require the utmost discretion and a solid pry-bar.

The pry-bar is a useful, I might say indispensable, implement to the modern housebreaker. It is a stout tool forged from Sheffield steel, curved into the shape of the letter *J*, with flat prongs at each extremity. These can be inserted into the narrowest crevice, and the operator can exert very considerable leverage—enough, if he has any muscle, to open any ordinary door or window. I do not include those doors or windows reinforced against just this sort of attack. Because of its compactness, one may easily conceal the pry-bar beneath an overcoat, wrapped in a hand towel for padding and hooked over the shoulder.

If the pry-bar has a disadvantage, it is that possession of such an implement is difficult to explain to the custodians of the Law. Whenever I have recourse to one, I borrow it from an acquaintance in the building trade that has legitimate cause for it. If one were discovered in my lodgings, questions might be asked.

My friend was obliging as ever and quickly extracted the said implement from his toolbox. "Now don't go doing anything I wouldn't do, Harry." He winked at me as he handed it over.

A man who is in debt but possesses some form of portable wealth is in a different situation to regular persons. He can't put it in the bank, or even keep it at home, because debt collectors, creditors, bailiffs, and others are most likely to look there. He has to hide his wealth away, like an old-time pirate burying his gold. Like the celebrated Captain Kidd, in fact, a man who Sir Ernest clearly admired in some of his capacities.

It is a matter of some interest in my line to observe how little we need to do protect things of value. The rule of law is so deeply ingrained that the mere suggestion of a barrier is sufficient to deter all but the most determined. Fences so low you can step over them defend our gardens, and even our front doors are made of flimsy wood that gives way to an insistent shoulder. Of course, stealth is also a consideration, which is why a pry-bar is a useful appendage for forcing a window. Breaking the glass attracts attention. Though of course plenty of thieves will break a plate-glass window with a hammer to get what they want.

The question then was where Sir Ernest would hide his putative valuables. Not at home, clearly, and perhaps not even with his mistress—with any of his mistresses. No, we are creatures of habit, and when we find a good hiding place, we tend to stick to it, even if it's from our childhood. I was to try my luck with Sir Ernest's oldest cache.

There was a good moon and a cold wind that night, both of which favoured me. The chill breeze meant few pedestrians were about, and nobody would look twice at a man in a heavy overcoat with his bowler hat pulled forward against the wind.

I glanced behind me once or twice. The guilty flee where none pursues, or so they say. If I had encountered a constable, I might have babbled like the most obvious guilt-wracked criminal. Fortunately, I saw none.

With the application of the pry bar to the chain, the locked side gate to the garden, popped open with a small metallic screech and little resistance. I tossed the broken lock aside, opened the gate, and stepped cautiously through.

The only illumination was the light from the sky, enough to find my way across the lawn to the square bulk of the summerhouse. That lock was broken, no need for the pry bar. Stepping inside onto floorboards, I closed the door behind me, feeling for the electric torch in my pocket.

In the almost absolute velvet darkness, I knew I was not alone. By that sixth sense which warns us a room is occupied before we even see the occupant, I felt a presence nearby. It was a chilling moment. I'm not afraid of anything I can see, but there was menace in the darkness. I felt like a grave robber at a haunted tomb.

I stayed motionless, not even breathing, trying not to give my position away. The other would have seen my silhouette and known where I was, but I hesitated to move for fear of making a sound. There was no blow, no shot, but I had the sense of being scrutinised in spite of the intense dark.

I brought the torch out and snapped it on. The circle of yellow light illuminated heavy garden chairs stacked together awkwardly, and a folded garden parasol. I swept it around the small room, and the shadows leaned and bent, forming suggestive shapes, but it revealed no human presence.

I breathed again, but oddly, the sense that I was not alone persisted. I swung the torch to and fro. Odd that a few shadows should scare one usually unmoved by physical danger!

The light fell on a narrow, oblong box that I took for a coffin, and I almost dropped the torch. Then I saw the lettering on it: "Harrison Bros: complete garden croquet set: mallets, hoops and balls: an entertainment for young and old." As harmless an object as you could imagine.

But still, I did not like the way the shadows moved. And while I could not hear any breathing, there was a kind of murmuring, so faint it might have been the rushing of my own blood, but it rose and fell like distant waves. It was not an external sound, and it was not internal, either. It was like the sound of a seashell held up to your ear.

My foot touched something on the floor. It was a wooden baton, of the type used by conductors or professors. I did not understand its presence. *Could it have fallen from above?*

I swallowed and felt the lump in my throat. With an awful sense of premonition, I slowly tilted the torch and looked upwards at the shape I sensed looming right over me. My mind had already formed an image of it, a huge spider with legs that spanned the width of the summerhouse, poised over me. Not quite a spider, but something that writhed... I forced myself to look upwards before the image could take shape and my imagination overwhelmed my courage.

There were plenty of cobwebs but no spiders, unless they were small ones. Nothing but the wooden struts supporting the roof that, at the edge of vision, might give the suggestion of a spider shape—at least to an impressionable eye in the dark.

I had half a mind to get out there and then. Instead, I steeled myself and followed the instructions, finding my way to the fourth floorboard from the left-hand wall. After looking about the place once more with the circle of light, I directed the torch to the floorboard and discovered the place where it was loose. Underneath it was an empty space and—yes!—a container. I reached in and pulled out a dusty old biscuit-tin.

The murmuring in my ears rose. As I whirled the torch about, the shadows whisked together for an instant before dispersing. An illusion, of course, but a disturbing one, and I left that summerhouse at some speed, the door banging behind me, the biscuit tin tucked firmly under my elbow. I was across the lawn and through the gate too, out on to the street and, as I thought, safety.

I stopped to catch my breath under a streetlight, exhaling streams of steam like a horse. The feeling of being watched, of another presence, was as strong as ever. I whirled around, but no one pursued me. Two workmen passed by on the other side, deep in conversation and passing a bottle between them, but that was all.

That nagging sense of another presence stayed with me as I walked on. I suspected it had to do with whatever was in that biscuit tin, as though a haunted thing, if that made any sense. My instructions had warned me not to open whatever container the hidey-hole concealed but to return it unopened to Mr Rowe. Perhaps it was a fragile thing he did not trust to my sausage fingers. More, perhaps, he was afraid the glittering prize would seduce me and I would refuse to give it up.

Or perhaps the treasure was in some way perilous.

The box did not feel like it contained a living thing. It did not grow warm. But there was a sense of... something. A boxer learns to trust his instincts, to dodge the punch a split second before his opponent's glove moves. And something about that box stirred my instincts down to the marrow of my bones. The big spider that loomed over me in the summerhouse was looming still, something watching me intently from a direction I could not fathom out.

Because I had the sense of that presence, I was slow to notice when someone came up behind me. I did not turn until the last second, just in time to see the blur of motion and the arc of an arm swinging towards me in the dark, followed by that jarring impact.

I have taken many blows to the head. The gloved fist and the naked fist have their own distinct sensations, as singular as the bouquet of claret or Beaujolais to the wine connoisseur. This, however, was the more powerful but slightly padded blow of a sandbag or blackjack. It caught me awkwardly but solidly enough to send me reeling and falling the long way down to the gently yielding turf, trailing, it seemed to me, a long stream of stars as I went.

Consciousness returned and I twisted, rolled, and rose to my feet, instinctively feeling for the ropes even though I was not in the ring. A painful lump on the side of my head mapped the blow's location, but there was no cut and no bleeding. A cold compress would help with the pain, but the humiliation would stay with me.

It was a great loss to be robbed just at the hour of my triumph, and yet I was not as downcast as I might have been. Some part of me was more than a little glad to be rid of whatever was in that tin. It might indeed be valuable, but it felt very dangerous, too dangerous for a man like Harry Stubbs to have in his possession.

Round Six: The Irishmen

As I came down to breakfast next morning, the landlady informed me a small boy was waiting to see me in the parlour at my leisure. He was to transmit his message only to me in person, she said, a trifle sniffily.

Going through, I recognised Arthur Renville's eldest, a fine-looking young chap of eleven years, sitting in a hard-backed chair as straight as a guardsman. He stood up and addressed me with the authority of a bonded messenger. "Begging your pardon, Mr Stubbs. If you come with me directly, you will learn something to your advantage."

"What would that be, then?"

"Can't tell you, sir."

"Where will you take me?"

"Can't tell that either, sir."

The boy had been well schooled.

"Just so," I said. "Young Renville, are you permitted to tell me if you have breakfasted yet?"

"No, sir—I mean yes, sir, I can tell you, and no, sir."

The fried eggs looked very tempting, and I was loathe to leave them. I requested the landlady make the toast up into a parcel of egg sandwiches sandwiches. She wrapped them in kitchen paper and passed them to Renville's boy while I pulled on my boots and buttoned up my coat.

It was a fine morning but sharp. There was no frost on the lawns. Shops were unfastening their shutters preparatory to opening, and clerks, labourers, and shop girls on their way to work filled the streets. The younger Renville led me rapidly up Central hill, towards Westow Hill. We continued for some minutes.

"Is it far? Hadn't we better get a cab?" I asked.

"No, sir. Cabbies tell tales."

We turned off down Woodland road then into a lane that terminated at a stableyard. Arthur Renville the elder stepped out of a stall, flicked a cigarette aside, and saluted us. "You hurry off home now," he told the boy. "You've done a good job. And remember—not a word to anyone, even Mother."

I relieved the boy of the parcel of sandwiches, passing him one. The lad dashed off at the double, eating as he went. I supposed he would be late for school, but only a brave teacher would punish Arthur Renville's boy without his permission.

"Morning, Arthur. What's the S.P.?"

"I think we've got your Irish," he said without the slightest humour or triumph in his voice. He led me into a straw-covered paddock. I was expecting to find them trussed up like chickens with Arthur's minions standing guard, but nobody was there. At least, nobody living. As I looked down, I saw with a shock the three of them, half buried in the straw, as lifeless as sacks. When I strode forward for a closer look, I received a second shock.

All three had been cleanly decapitated, the heads lying next to the bodies. The heads had fallen, or more likely been moved, so the faces were visible. I recognised at once three of my assailants from outside the Conquering Hero: the heavyweight Mickey, his associate who had tried to club me with so little success, and the one who had tried to run.

"What happened here? Who did this?"

"I wanted to ask you the same," said Renville. He looked down at the bodies with distaste. "This is highly irregular, Stubbsy, highly irregular indeed. I expected much better from you, really I did. I thought you was in a respectable trade now, not getting mixed up with murderers."

"This situation is none of my making," I protested.

"Isn't it, though? These men appear from thin air, with no purpose but assaulting your person, and then they show up again slaughtered like pigs, right on my patch. I can't see that this is nothing to do with you, however I try, and I did expect better." He let out a sigh and faced me. "In any case, the pertinent facts are these. Certain informants discovered that these men were camped out here—navvies and the like often use the place as informal accommodation. I approached personally last night with the intention of carrying out an interview and discovered this sorry scene you find here."

I continued to walk around, scrutinising the bodies from different angles, looking about them in the straw. "Were they beheaded post-mortem?"

"That would not seem to be the case." Arthur squatted beside me. "As near as I can tell it, Stubbsy, decapitation occurred coincident with and at the same time as actual death. But really! What kind of savages are you dealing with—Hottentots? Borneo head-hunters?"

He went on, and I lost track of his words. This was very strange indeed. I've done my time behind a butcher's counter, and I've seen meat cut, chopped, and sawed with a dozen instruments. I've seen it cut with sharp blades and blunt ones, by real masters and by raw apprentices. But no instrument I could recognise had cut those severed heads. The meat had been cut very cleanly, and the ends had an odd finish to them—pickled pork would be the closest comparison I could make, or perhaps seared. The meat had not been cooked but treated in some way.

"Stubbsy, what are you doing there?"

I twisted some straws together and poked at the vertebrae sticking out of Mickey's neck then inspected the matching end. I did the same with a second body. A cord of muscle and skin remained on one side as though the killer had not quite caught that one squarely. "Were they killed from in front or behind?" I asked.

"I don't know—why's it matter?"

"I don't know, either. The cut is perfectly even. You can't tell if it's left to right or front to back or what. If you were to have the sharpest blade in the world, you couldn't cut so cleanly. And it didn't cut the bone, neither, but it cut through the spinal cord inside the neck bone… how can that happen? Have you ever seen anything like this?"

"Don't look at me, Stubbsy."

"Maybe it was some sort of electrical saw, or surgical instrument," I said aloud.

"Or shrapnel."

I shook my head. I had spent the war lugging sixty-pound bursting shells, and we had suffered the effect of counter-battery fire by German fifteen-centimetre guns. One man might be decapitated, but not three, and the mess was far greater.

"Not much blood," Arthur added. He had calmed down now and was looking at it more rationally. "The straw soaked up what there was, but there wasn't much to begin with."

Something stirred in the straw, and I had the horrible impression that one of the heads was moving, working its jaws to speak something except it had no breath.

"Garn!" shouted Arthur, and a rat scuttled away through the straw. It had been chewing at the soft meat of the severed neck. "Vermin everywhere."

Then I saw the biscuit tin. It was open and lying empty a few feet away from one of the bodies. Next to it was a white object that proved to be a piece of crumpled tissue paper. There was, of course, no sign of what it had wrapped. I took both the tin and the tissue.

"This is only three of the men," I said. "What about the other?"

"He doesn't signify right now. What bothers me is these three dead 'uns here. Now, I'm going to make them disappear somewhere they won't easily be found. The last thing I want is police and murder investigations stirring things up—especially when it leads back to Harry Stubbs, known to be an acquaintance of mine."

"The police might think you'd arranged it. A sort of revenge for the attack outside the Hero."

"They might well suspect that," he said patiently. "And they might stumble over a few other things in their size nines while they were about it. So what I'm saying is, are you going to give me any more grief?"

"I hadn't the foggiest that this could happen. There's money at stake—perhaps thousands of pounds—but Mr Rowe never hinted there might be criminal gangs in it."

"I trust you." Arthur looked over the dismal scene. "But I think you should have a word with your Mr Rowe. I don't think he's playing straight with you. If the other one shows up, and I'm sure he will, you'll be the first to know."

"You're a pal, Arthur."

"Keep looking over your shoulder, Stubbsy. This ain't over yet."

ROUND SEVEN: THE MASTERMIND

ONCE MORE I SQUARED UP to write a report on my investigation and struggled with what to leave out and what to include. The failure of my attempts to retrieve Shackleton's treasure-box was one thing; the dead Irishmen were another matter entirely. In the end, I eschewed any attempt at picking and choosing and laid the whole thing before Mr Rowe to use his superior understanding and judgement, neglecting only mention of Arthur. The greatest danger, I surmised, was that I would omit a vital piece of evidence. If Mr Rowe wanted to go to the police, so be it.

All I had to show for my expedition was a piece of tissue paper and empty biscuit tin. The tin, from Huntley and Palmer, yielded no information, but the paper was more informative. The contents had perforce imprinted the wrapping. It was ordinary tissue paper, a type commonly used to wrap delicate clothing and other items, of double thickness, white in colour, of ordinary manufacture and not especially old. Judging from the creases, it had been folded up inside the box. I looked for crumbs or fibres and found nothing. I sniffed the paper, a faint residue of wood and dry earth.

I tried folding and refolding the paper and concluded it had wrapped a flat object perhaps five inches across with five equal projections. A medallion or ornament in the shape of a star. Perhaps a piece of jewellery—or a fossil.

By the end of the morning, I had completed my report. I submitted it to Mr Rowe, with the tissue paper as an enclosure duly noted, via Mrs Crawford. Fortunately, another matter relating to the repossession of a motorcar called me away, and my mind was distracted.

The murder—and it must have been murder—of the three Irishmen was a puzzle too deep for me. Obviously, one of them had coshed me and taken the box, and a third party had then taken it off them. But I could not even speculate whom they were working for, never mind who else may be involved.

The next day the office seemed livelier than usual, and I soon apprehended that Mrs Crawford was not at her desk. In her absence, the outer office took on the air of a schoolroom without a teacher. I found two messages waiting for me, one an office memorandum about the excessive use of vellum paper for unimportant documents. The other was from Mr Rowe and was most mysterious. It instructed me to make my way to the Upper Norwood recreation ground to a certain bench, where I would receive further instruction. I was on no account to let anyone else know where I was going.

It was a clear, bright morning, and the sun made a pretty show on the frost, but the wind was too sharp unless you were walking briskly. I passed housewives with baskets on their way to the shops, delivery boys on foot and on bicycle, a postman finishing his morning rounds, a group of children from the Blind School led in a crocodile by a teacher. The world was going about its regular business.

The Recreation ground was a large rectangular area consisting of playing fields at one end and a landscaped section at the other. Consulting my instructions, I located the bench directed. Nobody was in sight except a pair of municipal gardeners digging up flowerbeds in anticipation of spring. The ground was hard frozen, and that was an optimistic task.

"Good morning, Mr Stubbs," Mrs Crawford greeted me cordially and indicated I should remain seated. "A chilly morning, I'm afraid, but we need a secluded spot away from other ears." She was wearing a long coat trimmed with fur, patent leather shoes, a black hat, and carried a large handbag and a black umbrella. She remained standing as she spoke. Outside the office, she seemed different from her usual self. I had never seen her without her reading glasses. "This will be a morning of revelations. Firstly and most importantly, you are about to become a wealthy man—if you're able to follow my instructions."

"*Your* instructions?"

"Yes, mine. In fact, you've been following them for some time. That is one of the things about which I must undeceive you. I'm afraid the world is not as kind and generous a place as you have been led to believe," she said sadly. "Solicitors' firms are not apt to give golden opportunities to boxers with no qualifications and a taste for adventure stories. Mr Rowe has not been taking a personal interest in your career."

"Yes, he is," I protested automatically. "I have had many words of encouragement from him and some very flattering reports on my performance."

"I'm afraid not. You may have received messages in his name, but he wrote not one of them. Your employment as Latham and Rowe was entirely on my initiative. The partners believe you are kept on to help with debt collection duties and the like. They have no idea of the terms of your engagement. In effect, you have been working entirely for me."

This shocking news took some time to digest.

"My interest," Mrs Crawford went on, "is in the Shackleton case. Again, Mr Rowe has no idea the firm is still pursuing it. As far as he's concerned, it's a dead letter. Only you and I know otherwise."

"But Mrs Crawford, why?"

"Mr Stubbs, have you met a single person in your investigations who genuinely believed that Shackleton had anything of value? I think not. The world is persuaded that he was nothing but a wild adventurer, a treasure-hunter who never found treasure. But we know different. We know he found Aladdin's cave."

"How do we know that? And what did he find? What was in that biscuit tin?"

"That is the answer to the mystery and the gold at the end of the rainbow. I will explain more at the proper time. The only question now is whether you are willing to walk the final mile with me and claim the reward for your labours."

I considered the proposition, tried to gauge what she was asking of me and what was at stake. "My position at Latham and Rowe," I started.

"Put it out of your mind." She shook her head. "I have submitted my resignation, 'for personal reasons' with immediate effect and it has been accepted. I have destroyed the paperwork relating to the Shackleton legacy. If you go back, you will not have a post, and there are likely to be some difficulties over your employment there. Our bridges are well and truly burned, Mr Stubbs. We must look forward."

The mention of Shackleton's name made me think of him and the Imperial Trans-Antarctic *Endurance* Expedition in 1914. When the *Endurance*, had been stuck in the ice for months, and then crumpled like an empty tin can, Shackleton's dream of crossing the Antarctic disappeared – the pressing matter then was how they could ever get home alive.

The gardeners had dug two rows, and in that time, my dream of being a lawyer's clerk sank. What of my life I could salvage? "You mentioned wealth," I said.

"Yes. Again, I can explain more later. But you may trust me when I say there will be more money than you can imagine." Mrs Crawford's eyes were steely blue, and she had a quality about her you might call resolution. If she were a man, she might have been a leader.

"It is not that I doubt you, but I feel a more thorough explanation of how this wealth is to be obtained, and the legalities of the situation, are in order."

Mrs Crawford blinked. "Legalities? Mr Stubbs, we are to retrieve some property which rightfully belongs to the Shackleton estate, and which was stolen—with violence, I might add—from you yourself. As we are still acting pro tem for Latham and Rowe, we are entirely on the side of the law. And I assure you the finder's fee will be a king's ransom at the least."

The proposition had become much simpler. I was to continue acting just as before, in pursuit of Shackleton mysterious treasure. "Why have you told me this?" I said at last. "Why not just issue another letter under Mr Rowe's name?"

"Firstly, because I need to be part of the expedition. Secondly, because you will become party to some extraordinary information, and I wish you to be prepared for it."

The prospect of vast wealth, and getting a little of my own back on the individual who struck me from behind, both enticed me. But the lure of adventure really drew me on. The same that lures a man to step into the ring, heedless of the risk that he will be beaten black and blue. "Will you at least tell me why we may not conduct matters through the usual channels for recovering stolen property from a malefactor?"

"When you sensed a presence in the summerhouse, it was no illusion. And those misfortunate Irishmen did not die by any normal means, as you must realise. "

"Who killed them?"

"Not who but what. A force that the regular authorities are singularly ill equipped to deal with. You needn't frown so, Mr Stubbs. I have my own sources of intelligence, and I'm confident of bringing matters to a successful conclusion. If," she added, "you are with me. That will mean following my instructions promptly and without question."

"I can do that."

"I was sure you could. You will hear some very strange things this morning. I want you to ignore them as far as possible, and keep your attention riveted to the men with whom we are dealing. They are exceptionally dangerous. Take your eyes off them, and we'll both have our throats cut."

Her frank language took me aback. Mrs Crawford was not at all the woman I had taken her to be. She might have been Boudicca, with the sun glinting from her auburn pompadour under her hat.

"I am with you," I said at length.

"Good man. Now, may I ask you to fetch a cab and meet me at the entrance to the park here?"

"Very good, Mrs Crawford."

I hurried off with a strange feeling of exhaltation. I was not looking back to the ruined career behind me; I was looking forward to the encounter to come with the prospect of danger and riches. The sun was sparkling on the frosty lawns, and I was gambling everything. I believe I might have started whistling.

ROUND EIGHT: THE COLLECTOR

WE LEFT THE CAB TWO streets away from our destination. Mrs Crawford walked ahead of me at a smart pace, swinging her rolled umbrella purposefully. I followed with slow strides, one step to her two.

"You recognise the address?" she asked, stopping outside a town house with a brass knocker in the shape of a fist. The area had once been respectable but was now less so; I knew it well from my debt-collecting days, knew how little money there was on this street. A curtain across the road jerked.

"The collector," I said. "The one who buys anything Shackleton touched."

"Exactly. Harcourt is his name. We require the element of surprise, so I'll ask you to break the door down, if you please, Mr Stubbs."

Doors, as I have said, have a largely symbolic value in repelling intruders. That said, some are more stoutly secured than others are. I put my fingertips close to the jamb, gauging its strength and where it was bolted. I took a half step back and directed a kick at the lock.

The deadbolt was all that held it; at my impulse, the door flew open. Metal fittings clattered on the stone floor beyond.

"The bailiffs have come and they mean to collect," declared Mrs Crawford, stepping over the threshold into the bare, shadowy hall. I judged it cheap accommodation, left unfurnished. "Mr Stubbs, kindly intercept anyone who attempts to interfere."

She had barely spoken these words when a man in shirtsleeves and braces came through a doorway to my right. He grabbed a walking stick leaning in one corner, but before he could fully raise it, I hit him with a straight left to the abdomen, a right to his chin, and a left to the side of his face. It was instinctive boxing but sound. When you work the drills long enough, the combinations come out right without having to think. He was only a small man, and it was a clean knockout.

I recognised my would-be assailant from the fight outside the pub. The fourth of the Irishmen, the man with the knife. No wonder his face was bruised.

"His name is Connell, and he's a criminal known to the police," said Mrs Crawford. "Keep hold of him."

I patted him for a knife and found nothing. We had caught him unprepared.

Then she turned and called up the stairs in a ringing voice, "Good morning. I am Mrs Geraldine Crawford, from the firm of Latham and Rowe of upper Norwood, representing the creditors to the estate of the late Sir Ernest Shackleton. I have reason to believe that you are in possession of property pertaining to the estate, and I wish to discuss the matter."

"You had better come upstairs, then," came the quiet reply.

We could not see the speaker, who was up on the second landing. Mrs Crawford indicated I bring the man who had attacked me; I half-dragged, half-carried him, and we went upstairs at a brisk pace.

A tall, sandy-haired gentleman with a moustache greeted us on the landing. He was wearing a good tweed suit and a watch chain. I would have said he was fifty.

"Roger Harcourt," she said.

"Geraldine Crawford," said the other. "And I'd like to mention that if you attempt violence, my associate will be forced to restrain you."

I must have cut a menacing figure, coming out of the shadows and tossing aside the still-stunned Connell with one hand. He took a step back.

"Purely a precaution," Mrs Crawford went on. "I do want to talk to you, Mr Harcourt, and I don't want you doing anything precipitate to prevent our talking."

"Indeed." Harcourt showed us in to a room furnished sparsely and rather cheaply with second-hand items. A bachelor's room, the study or workroom of a man with varied interests. A side table held decanters and a dozen glasses, none of them clean. An odd assortment of old books, well bound and perhaps valuable, packed the shelf behind him, but nothing else in the room indicated wealth or taste.

The large table at one end, which I instantly identified as a collection of items relating to Sir Ernest, was the room's most remarkable feature. There were skis, winter coats, travelling chests, an ice axe hanging from its leather thong, even pairs of snowshoes like crude tennis rackets.

Harcourt scowled at Connell, who took a seat in the corner. I went to search Harcourt for weapons, but Mrs Crawford indicated it would not be necessary. He sat behind the desk, and we sat in front of it in mismatched easy chairs, as though we had come into his office to make a request.

The desk was spread with an unusual display of impedimenta: a wooden case of jewellers' screwdrivers, a long wooden pointer, a corkscrew, a penny whistle, a magnifying lens, an old hearing trumpet, a candle and matches, and a many-bladed pocketknife with a scaling instrument extended. I thought of the tray of assorted items in Kim's game. Only the ashtray full of cigar stubs made sense. A notebook, a couple of books whose titles I could not see, and a scrap of ancient leather marked with a five-sided pattern or picture, also lay there.

"Mr Harcourt is the younger brother of Sir Edward Harcourt of Effra Hall," Mrs Crawford informed me.

"He was a friend of Ernest Shackleton for some years. Mr Harcourt, this is my associate, Mr Stubbs."

Knowing who he was, I could see his type. The younger brother, a man without any trade, profession, or prospects. He had to make his way by means of his social connections and the opportunities and knowledge they afforded. I knew his sort as gamblers, at the ring and the racetrack. A few of them were always about. They patronised fighters or owned shares in horses. Many of them played cards with those who could afford to lose. Harcourt's face showed signs of years of late nights and drinking. Judging from his surroundings, I would say he was not a successful gambler.

Harcourt's gaze barely flicked over me, as though I was merely a hired thug. A more sensitive man might have been insulted, but his assumption was understandable, especially given the state of his front door.

For my part, I belatedly recognised him as the man with the bushy beard in the train from Chichester and in the Conquering Hero. The beard was a false stage prop, no doubt.

"What may I do for you, Mrs Crawford?" he asked, completely composed. "You must have a good reason for forced entry into a man's house."

"Let us start with the piece of property you took from Mr Stubbs last night."

Harcourt had the nerve to raise an eyebrow quizzically. "Exactly what property would that be? It's well known that I pay for any souvenirs of Shackleton, so perhaps someone was hoping to get something they could sell to me. I hope that Connell and his disreputable friends didn't rob you." He looked over to the bruised man. "I wouldn't know anything about it."

"There are three dead men at a stables this morning," said Mrs Crawford, changing tack. "I know how they died."

"Indeed?"

The faint smile about his lips troubled me. I had not expected that type of interview. Harcourt was likely a murderer, but Mrs Crawford was chatting as politely as though he was a social acquaintance.

"They died by the disruption of protein molecules by resonant radio waves," she said coolly. "Proteins bind together our muscles, ligaments, and other connective tissue. If the molecular bonds within them are broken, they lose their strength. Tissue under tension will part. A narrow beam of radio waves can cut through such tissue like a hot knife through butter. Even to the degree of beheading a man."

He nodded slowly, evidently re-appraising her. "Needless to say, it was not my doing. They were warned. But like Pandora, they heedlessly opened the box. Connell and I arrived five minutes too late."

"Mr Waters died the same way."

"You are well-informed," he said.

"I had his body dug up especially. The damage to his skull was most unusual."

"Didn't have too many brains in the first place," said Harcourt drily. "He was another greedy fool. He could have saved me two years if he'd have told me what he was doing."

I had not heard of Mr Waters. I later learned he had died in the Greyhound public house two years previously.

"You didn't bring the police, so I assume you can only have come for one reason. How much do you want?"

She shook her head. "I believe we can work together. I think we have the same aim."

"What makes you think I need your assistance?" Harcourt demanded.

"Because you are not yet seated on a golden throne playing with a bowl of diamonds the size of goose eggs."

"Ha! Quite so... but I repeat my question. How can you help?"

It seemed to me that we were in a position to demand our property. But Harcourt felt otherwise, and Mrs Crawford evidently agreed, as she did not simply order him to hand over the object of our quest. These two believed some sort of cerebral sparring was necessary.

"I can help you realise the value of what you have."

"I've a half-share in this," said Connell. "So you're dealing with me as well."

Mrs Crawford turned her gaze on him. "Do you actually know what it is you have, or has Mr Harcourt kept that to himself?"

"It's a container for valuables," said Connell. "And it's worth a pile of money. But it's booby-trapped."

She waited, but he had nothing more to add. As Mrs Crawford had guessed, he was as ignorant as I was. Connell and I were the corner men in this bout. We had nothing to do but watch the match between our principles, who were still finding their distance.

"Let me tell you my story," she said.

"Some years ago, an Oxford professor of classical studies was looking into the antecedents of Homer's odyssey. As you might know, there are several incidents—the Cyclops, the lotus-eaters, the Old Man of the Sea—which are common to the *Odyssey* and the voyages of Sinbad in the *Arabian Nights*. Some believe the stories migrated from Greece to Arabia; the professor believed the opposite. He gathered many versions of the stories, and as he did so, he noted various correspondences and changes over time."

Harcourt was leaning forward, nodding. Mrs Crawford was not the dragonish woman who reigned in the office but someone I did not recognise.

"It was his theory that the tales referred, albeit in distorted form, to some historical events. He collected more and more versions of these stories and became convinced that both Ali Baba's and Aladdin's cave referred to the same place. As you may be aware, Galland and Hammer-Purgstall did not take those stories from the original *Arabian Nights* but derived them from another Arabic book known to occultists. In the *Nights*, we find repeated references to an abandoned remnant of an unknown civilization, which also appears as the City of

Brass, Irem, the City of Pillars and others. These cities are greater than anything ever seen. Adventurous men tried to plunder them… and unsleeping mechanical guardians sliced some of them to pieces.

"The professors's findings were detailed and comprehensive, and he was roundly mocked for them. After *The Golden Bough*, the academics were more jealous of their domain than ever. This sort of intrusion from folklore goes hard. Of course, that only strengthened his belief, and the professor gathered even more material from ever more obscure sources. These included that occult Arabic work which is entirely discreditable—I think you know what I am referring to. Naturally, attempts to present his thesis were met with increasing hostility. He died without finding a publisher for his great manuscript, and in the end, only one person read the completed version . His secretary, who decided to pursue her own investigation."

"I begin to grasp your situation," said Harcourt.

"Historians do not yet accept the professor's lost cities, but there are myths, legends, and rumours. There is one continent yet to be explored and a certain Turkish map, with which you are surely acquainted, pointing to it. A wild Irish adventurer like Ernest Shackleton might be persuaded to the quest—if someone were to put him up to it.

"I looked through the explorers' account and found some peculiarities in Shackleton's descriptions, in particular the unseen presence that walked with him during the *Endurance* expedition – you know *The Waste Land?* Unfortunately, he was dead by then. I insinuated myself into the office of the solicitors managing his estate by forging a few references. "

"Was there a convenient vacancy just then, or did you create one?" Harcourt asked. "While we're at it, what did your professor die of exactly?"

She ignored the questions, though she flushed slightly. "And that was when I started running across your trail. Wherever something related to Shackleton, there was your name. I made some enquiries. Your family goes back a long way, Mr Harcourt, and it has a particular reputation. I found about your friendship with Shackleton, and I saw you must be the one who guided him to look for traces of lost cities."

"Shackleton's expeditions never looked for any such things," I objected. "Nor found them." Even as I said it, I recalled the chimerical Fata Morgana described by Sir Ernest and by Brown.

"Shackleton knew better than to broadcast that aspect of his mission," said Mrs Crawford. "He never was a true gentleman, not as far as the Royal Geographical Society or His Majesty's government were concerned. He was no Robert Scott. If there was the prospect of real plunder, they wouldn't have given him a sniff of it."

"He was an adventurer," said Harcourt. "A man who would risk everything in pursuit of a glimmer dream where others could only see icy wastes."

"You're Abanezar," I said.

"I beg your pardon?"

"The sorcerer who pretends to be Aladdin's uncle. He knew where the lamp was, but he couldn't get it. Only Aladdin could do that, so Abanazer used him."

"And Shackleton, and a few of those with him, did penetrate to some sort of ancient ruin somewhere in the ice," said Mrs Crawford. "A remote outpost, like a lighthouse or a shepherds hut, but still a momentous discovery greater than the Valley of the Kings—and just as rich in its way. All they could bring back was what they could carry in their pockets. That was our biggest enigma, wasn't it, Stubbs? What would a man bring back if he did find Aladdin's cave?"

"What indeed?" asked Harcourt. "Does your assistant know what he's been risking his life for?"

"In Aladdin's cave," said Mrs Crawford, "the most valuable item is not the pots of gold, or the fat jewels like coloured fruit. The most valuable item is"—she looked to me to finish the sentence.

"Aladdin's lamp."

"Indeed," said Harcourt. "But what does that mean?"

"It is obvious," Mrs Crawford said, I think for Harcourt's benefit. "The fruits of science are the most valuable thing a society could produce. Not art, because art has no value outside of its place of origin. Oriental art means little to us. But machinery has a universal value."

"But what sort of machinery could you put in your pocket?" Harcourt challenged.

"Ancient Rome would not be impressed our gold and jewels," said Mrs Crawford. "They already have plenty of those. But a pocket watch, or a magnetic compass—those would be beyond the price of rubies, because the Romans never had anything like them. Imagine what wonders you could show them with a folding telescope. A barometer to forecast the weather would make you a greater prophet than the Sibyls. And in a city whose science was as far in advance of ours as we are in advance of Rome, they would have devices you could carry in your pocket, which might astound the world. Like our many-bladed pocket companions with a dozen tools but far more advanced."

"Such as a portable wireless telephone," I said. "Which was also a telescope."

Harcourt gave me a startled look, as though a piece of furniture had spoken.

"A radio set which is more than just a radio," she went on. "A device which both receives and transmits every form of electromagnetism. It might function as an electric lamp—or it could take X-ray photographs of your body and treat infections with healing radiations. Perhaps it could fill your muscles with energy so you have no need for food. That could send a telegraphic message to Australia or pluck knowledge from any library or newspaper office out of thin air. Navigate anywhere the surface of the earth by its magnetic field, like a bird—or transmit a fine beam that cuts flesh like a scimitar."

Harcourt was nodding and smiling to himself at this litany.

"But how do you control such a device with so many different and complex operations?" she asked. "The most advanced science would produce the simplest possible means of control. Instead of hundreds of buttons and dials and levers, you have a servant who you command, by words and gestures, to carry out your will. A projection in the form of a willing slave—the Slave of the Lamp."

"A genie," I said aloud.

"Though the device is only described as a lamp in Aladdin. More often, it's a brass cucurbit marked with Solomon's seal. But it works through a sort of automaton that ignorant people might mistake for a genie. Or a devil."

"Rawmaish," said Connell. "Who are you trying to make a fool of?"

I recalled a scene in *Nanook of the North*, in which a singing voice from a gramophone baffles the Eskimo. That must have seemed like magic to him. And surely, a device made by some vastly more advanced civilisation would seem just as wondrous to us.

"Shackleton found just such a lamp, although, like Aladdin, he never knew the value of what he had. For him it was only important because it proved there was an ancient civilization. He wanted to go back and uncover a city, and he never gave up that hope."

"He betrayed me," said Harcourt. "He denied he ever found anything."

"You tried to trick him, and he fooled you. And after he died, you started buying up anything of his that might have something secreted in it." She gestured to the collection on the other side of the room. "Coats, skis, furniture. 'New lamps for old'—but you never showed an interest in buying his papers. That was how I knew you were looking for the same object as me."

"She's a clever one," said Connell.

She was probing, not wishing to give too much away but knowing she needed to move to get the other to respond. "I've done some work. You know my credentials now. But before I say more, Mr Stubbs and I need to know whether we're merely dealing with a clever thief, or do you truly know where the lamp came from and how to command it?"

Harcourt considered the question a long minute. I did not like the situation. Both he and Connell were dangerous men, and calculations beyond my ken were taking place. The gambler weighed the situation then played his card.

"This lost city isn't just five thousand years old or yet fifty thousand." He looked from me to Connell and back. "It was an old, old place five hundred thousand years ago. You know what that means? No, I can see you do not. What that means is that these ancients weren't human. They were an amphibious race that built their empire millions of years before man was ever thought of. What do you think of that?"

"I'll take my share of the trim now," said Connell.

"You see," snapped Harcourt. "You're too ignorant to begin to understand the truth."

"What kind of race were they?" I suspected I might know already.

"You've already seen them, or their relatives," said Mrs Crawford. "They are tardigrades. The slow walkers."

"Tardigrades are minute."

"Their ancestors were. But so were ours. They evolved before the dinosaurs, but they left no fossils."

"They are the long sleepers," said Harcourt loudly, as if delivering a political speech. "Their civilisation endured so long because whenever conditions deteriorated—a famine, or an ice age or some other cataclysm, or barbarians at the gates—they simply hibernate for a few millennia. They secrete themselves in their tombs while the earth purges itself of its toxins and recovers its vitality, or while the barbarians die off, and they wake to a new, refreshed world. They rebuild their cities in a matter of months with the aid of cyclopean labourers that they manufacture synthetically."

"More genies," scoffed Connell.

"No, not genies—and you'd not laugh if you saw one," said Harcourt. "The ancients have no machinery, just monstrous living machines. All their vast libraries are condensed into what Mrs Crawford is pleased to call 'lamps'."

"What happened to them?" I asked.

"Can you still not understand? Nothing happened to them. 'That is not dead which can eternal lie.' The

Ancients are sleeping yet beneath the great ice sheets, under the oceans and in the bowels of the Earth. Fifty thousand years might seem a long while to you, but for them it's a pause no more significant than Parliament going into recess. No more than a good night's sleep. But I tell you, they will awake."

"And certain people are waiting for them," said Mrs Crawford.

Harcourt looked up sharply.

"The ancients domesticated human beings during their last period of wakefulness," she went on. "Certain families still remember their loyalty to those that sleep in the hills, and they guard the old magic. But I suppose that all the knowledge and power descends to your elder brother, and you do not inherit anything."

"I suppose not." Harcourt showed his teeth. "Primogeniture is not kind to younger brothers."

"Alas," she said, "some of us are left to make our own way in the world, to take what we can find."

They say that two thieves in the night always recognise each other. There might have been some understanding between Harcourt and Mrs Crawford, but Connell and I were still shut out.

"Play your stupid game," said Connell. "But I'm still getting my money."

"I'm owed something, too," I added, just for the sake of saying something. In truth, I craved explanation and inclusion in the conspiracy more than cash.

"This is more important than money," said Harcourt. "I want to save the British Empire from ruination."

At that moment, I began to doubt his sanity, if I had not before. And Mrs Crawford, whose sanity I never doubted, seemed to be playing him, provoking him further into madness.

"What ruination?" she asked.

"Don't you read the papers? We've been slipping for decades, and the last do practically exhausted us. The Americans and the Germans produce more coal and steel than we do. Communist Russia and Japan are growing fast, and China... but here, home rule for Ireland, India's next. Bits of the empire falling away like limbs off a leper."

"All empires fail eventually," said Mrs Crawford. "Rome, the Ottomans, the Moghuls."

"All human empires," corrected Harcourt. "But not theirs. Their empire has never fallen and never will. They sleep through the bad times and then they come back again, stronger than ever. The life of a human empire is like a day to them. If they become decadent over the course of a few thousand years, they sleep it off like a man recovering from a bender. They don't become degenerate as we are doing."

"What's that to us?" I asked.

"We are savages on the margins of a great empire," he said hotly. "When they return, we can be their allies—we, the British. Like the Iceni when the Roman came, or the Princely States today in India. The Ancients are largely an underwater race; they won't care much about what happens on land. We'll give them a few islands for trading ports, like Hong Kong and Singapore are to us. And then see what we do to the Germans and the Americans and the French! Let me pick up a wireless telephone, and I'll soon get through to the exchange and set the bells ringing. Wake up the sleepers."

Connell snorted. As an Irishman, he might have had different views on the worth of Empire. Perhaps Shackleton, another Irishman, did too.

"We share the same aim," said Mrs Crawford. "I see it as a new Renaissance throughout ancient knowledge. In the fifteenth century, the rediscovery of a few Greek manuscripts in the Arabic transformed civilisation. What could we not do together with the knowledge of the ancients?" Her words were encouraging, but there was a false note.

"You break my door down and attack my colleague. Somehow I don't feel inclined to trust you."

"Then trust this," Mrs Crawford said. She removed her gloves and showed her right hand, on which was ring with a tiny green stone shaped like a star. "The Seal of Solomon was originally a five-pointed star, not the six-pointed one of modern occultists. The Seal used to bind and control genies."

Harcourt's eyes widened.

"By God," he said. "My ring!"

"Your ring? Like the lamp, the ownership is open to debate. I rather think your brother would say you stole it from him. I borrowed it from Shackleton's estate."

"Give it to me."

"It is enough that it is in the room. What matters is that it will allow us to approach the lamp more safely."

Harcourt's eyes fixed on that ring for a long moment; somehow he tore his gaze off it and assumed his former manner. "That changes everything," he said. He opened a drawer on his desk. I jumped up, fearing he was going for a weapon, but he merely smiled and produced an object wrapped in a white silk handkerchief. "I believe this is what you've come for."

ROUND NINE: THE SLAVE OF THE LAMP

HE UNWRAPPED IT CAREFULLY. TO my eyes, it looked just like a green starfish. A perfect five-pointed star the colour of corroded brass, covered in irregular pits, which he passed over to Mrs Crawford.

A powerful sense of presence I had experienced in the summerhouse returned, as though another person had entered the room. The others seemed unaware of it.

"A star made of green stone," she said. "Exactly how he described it. Three years I've been looking for this."

"Twenty years it's taken me."

She put on her spectacles. "It's covered in tiny dots, in groups of five. Little pits, and nubs. And they keep changing."

"Like ticker tape in Braille," said Harcourt. "Stock market prices, or weather reports, or cricket scores."

"Very lovely," said Connell. "But while you two are spinning your fairy tales, me and you man Stubbs here want our money. Remember what you promised me."

Harcourt took a key from his watch chain and removed a substantial leather wallet from a locked drawer. He carelessly pulled out a huge bundle of notes and threw them down. "Eighteen hundred pounds, the last time I counted." He yanked some gold sovereigns from his pocket and tossed them down with so much force that one rolled from the table. "There, that's all I have in the world. I don't need it now. The two of you can share it out between you and go. We have business to do."

I'd never seen more money in one place, even in a bank. The big white notes made quite a pile. I attempted to calculate what it would be in months or years of salary but failed. Harcourt was a better gambler, or a less honest one, than I had thought.

"They're mad as hatters," Connell said mildly to me, stuffing a pile of folded notes in his back pockets and preferring the other half.

"I'm not going until I see the finish of this."

"Please yourself."

When I made no move to take the money, he changed tack. Even Connell, the shrewd, sharp-eyed criminal, the calculating man who took nobody's word, must have been a little taken by the thought of the *Arabian Nights'* treasures, or as Mellors put it, the leprechauns' gold at the end of the rainbow.

He knew about the dead men, and the risk that the thing might blow up in our faces. But by the very token of those deaths, some power must have been at work. A power that might make him far richer than a paltry few hundred pounds in banknotes.

"Sure, and I'll stay a little longer," he said. "Just to see if the horse runs, as the man said."

"You shall see." Harcourt rose from his chair and took up the pointer. He swished it in the air theatrically as he came around the desk. "Indeed you shall."

Mrs Crawford handed the star back to him. Harcourt placed it on the floor in the middle of the room and the four of us stood around it. Mrs Crawford was entranced, but I was on my guard. I sensed, as a boxer can, that he had made a false move. Misdirection was afoot, but I was too slow to see what it was. Harcourt passed the wand over the star. I watched his moves closely. The tip of the wand inscribed a five-pointed shape, as though he was drawing a pentagram in the air.

Black sparkles filled the air. At this point in theatre, there is a flash and a bang, and the genie appears in a cloud of smoke through a hidden trapdoor. The original story described the genie emerging in a cloud of smoke from the lamp. Neither was a faithful representation, but they were close.

The sparkles became larger, expanding like soap bubbles black and shiny as coal, fusing together into a single column of dark foam. Quite suddenly, the foam took on shape and the surface melted into a continuous, seamless skin.

A grey shadow rather than an object, but a shadow with three dimensions, filled the space between us. It was not a projection but a solid thing that cast a shadow by the electric light. If smoke was condensed and solidified, you could call it smoke, but it was like nothing I ever saw.

It moved, and I saw with a shock that it was a living thing.

"Behold," said Harcourt with grim pride. "The genie of the lamp."

Connell crossed himself.

"Don't make any sudden moves," said Harcourt. "Even with the ring, it might become hostile."

The best way I can describe it is to say it was like a big, thick tree stump the size of a barrel. After a second, branches emerged from it with leaves like palms, others long and bare, waving as if in a wind. It did not have a real head with identifiable features, but what might be seaweed crowned it. The colour of it was wrong, like a black-and-white photograph of a thing rather than the thing itself. The surface or skin was not like bark or scales but reminded me of lumpy pig's liver.

That bare description fails to convey the horror of its sudden appearance. It was as obscene as a lump of glistening excrement on a silk cushion, as obscene as waking to find a giant slug oozing over your pillow. For an instant, I almost bolted from the room. But I could look at it differently, sort of push it away from my mind.

If I viewed it not as a living thing but just as a tree stump with branches that twisted and curled in the wind, it was not so strange and unnatural as all that. It resembled Dr Evans' tardigrades, but only slightly. I might add also that I had the impression of the smell of the sea; not the actual smell, you understand, but the impression of it.

"The colouring is peculiar." Harcourt spoke in an odd, breathless tone as though barely keeping himself in check. I knew then that he was half-crazed, but I did not know what to do. "I believe their eyes see a different spectrum to ours, so the reproduction is imperfect."

"My... goodness..." was all Mrs Crawford could say. She was captivated, but she held up the ring like a shield in front of her. Connell seemed paralysed by the sight of it. Harcourt was strangely exultant.

A rich, alien music, like underwater birdsong, filled the room. It seemed to come from the walls. Harcourt took up the penny whistle from the desk and played a simple tune of several notes.

The music sounded again, exactly the same trilling birdsong.

"The whistle is inspired, but you do not quite have the correct grammar," said Mrs Crawford. "Still, I think we can work our way through and claim the slave of the sound."

In the tale of *Ali Baba and the Forty Thieves*, Ali Baba's brother dies because he does not pronounce the magic words "Open Sesame." Words are very important for commanding genies. Suppose you find the wonderful lamp, and you can compel the genie to offer you your three wishes. But suppose the genie has been in the lamp not since the days of Solomon the Wise but for fifty thousand years, when no human language existed. What language would it ask you in, and how could you reply? A language of music and waving gesture unknown to anyone alive. But perhaps scholars could piece some of it together, and perhaps two of the most astute scholars of that lost language were here.

Mrs Crawford whistled three notes, two long and one short.

The stump shuffled around, apparently looking for which of us had addressed it. It scrutinized each of us in turn, and I shuddered as those branches, too much like tentacles, waved towards me. The attention was too much for Connell. As soon as it faced him, he bolted and ran for the door

The thing jerked and hissed like escaping steam under high pressure. I watched in horror as it separated Connell's head from his body in mid-stride. There was no blade, not even a flash of light, just that sharp sound. The flesh seemed to part of its own accord, seething and splitting as if cut by an invisible scimitar. Connell's headless, lifeless body crumpled to the floor.

The thing hesitated then shuffled on, aiming itself at me. Mrs Crawford made to whistle but no sound came out. Without warning Harcourt seized the clasp knife from the desk, unfolded the longest blade, and stabbed Mrs Crawford in the chest. He plunged the blade in as far as it would go and twisted. Mrs Crawford's mouth opened in silent horror. She brought her hand up and he took it, feeling for the finger with the ring.

I acted without thinking, leaping to Mrs Crawford's defence and grappling with Harcourt. I'm no wrestler, but I know well the arts of physical restraint. He was an athletic man once, but I had thirty years' youth and four stones weight on him, and my training regime is unbroken. I held his forearms, but his strength was a phenomenon. My attempts to take him in a wrestling hold were fruitless.

"I must have the ring," spat Harcourt, struggling in my hands.

Mrs Crawford was lying where she fell, the knife still in her breast. The shadow-genie lurched at the edge of my vision.

"Murderer," I cried.

Suddenly Harcourt's hands were at my throat, and though his fingers could barely encircle my neck, his grip was crushingly powerful. I never knew a man so strong. Something huge and dark loomed beside us; I jerked away, more from revulsion than a fighter's impulse. There was an awful hissing like an enraged tomcat, and the pressure on my throat vanished.

Harcourt held up his two arms, hands neatly severed at the wrist, the ends cauterised, in front of his face. I could only stare in fascination.

"I must have the ring," he said again. He crouched down to paw at Mrs Crawford's body with his handless stumps.

I backed away until I felt the desk behind me.

Harcourt looked up at the thing towering over him. He held Mrs Crawford's hand between his stumps. "I am a Harcourt, and I have the ring," he said, wildly triumphant. "You cannot harm me!"

It flicked a branch in an odd gesture, and I looked away as that terrible steam-blast sounded again. The hollow thud of something hard on the wooden floor followed it.

The shadow-shape moved to face me, though it did not have a face. It was just the two of us now. My paralysis broken, I dropped into a fighting stance. I was weaving left and then right, ducking low. I suppose most people would have made a break for it, but I've never been a running man. Harry Stubbs doesn't turn his back on danger.

We shuffled around each other. I was working on instinct. You can think too much in the rings and tie yourself in knots. You just have to trust your gut feelings and get in there with all you can. That was one of those times.

My opponent, more awkward than any human boxer was, moved with geriatric awkwardness, like a seal or other sea-creature on land. When it stopped moving, I bobbed low, correctly anticipating the hissing guillotine noise that followed a moment later. The blow did not connect, and I danced away.

Like a boxer, it aimed its blows at the head, or more exactly the neck, so lively movement could make it miss its aim. A boxer, if he is any better than poor Mickey, quickly learns to adapt his punches to the opponent and anticipate dodges. I could only hope this thing would not recalibrate itself too quickly. If it simply changed its aim to my body, it might split me down the middle as easily as my father halves chickens with a cleaver.

You cannot win a fight with footwork and dodging, however expert. I needed to close and land some punches. Normally, I would have taken any opening, but I confess my opponent's inhuman physiognomy daunted me. The signs that would trigger my attack—a lowered guard, a head left unprotected—were absent. Also, the thing was a solid mass and that surface looked hard. Punching a tree trunk full force with an ungloved fist would be an error. That crowning mass of waving seaweed might be a weak spot, but it might be no more than the hair on a human head.

I feinted a step to the left and went right then forward. I had resolved to think of the thing as a punch bag and try a short combination of high and low blows against what might be the head and the body.

It was not as solid as a tree, nor as yielding as a bag or a human being. I sensed I had hit a great solid mass, but somehow it did not offer proper resistance and my arm snapped out to full reach as I punched right through it. I jumped back instinctively. I was hitting something both there and not there at the same time, the illusion of substance rather than the genuine article. An illusion cannot stop a fist. Fine black powder that dissolved like snow coated my hand.

Inevitably, I had laid myself open to a counterpunch. I ignored the rules of balance and guard, pushing off sideways from the desk as hissing filled the room. A whirling blade brushed my face, but that was all.

I almost tripped over Harcourt's body. I steadied myself on his chair then continued the movement and whipped the chair up, tossing it at the shadow shape while capering off to the side. The chair passed through it as through a ghost or a shadow. It stirred like smoke, but the gap reformed with black foaming. The genie showed no sign even of noticing, let alone discomposure from my attack.

When one plan of action fails, you must not despair but formulate another. That I learned from Sir Ernest. I did not stop moving but danced this way and that, searching for something that might help me. The ring on Mrs Crawford's finger might be a charm against it, but I feared I would be dead long before I could retrieve it—if I could even wear it, as my fingers were so much larger than hers.

I was looking for Harcourt's wand with some thought that I could dispel the thing by a reversal of the actions he had carried out. Instead, I saw the ice axe, and it brought an idea. That was more in my line than magic tricks, if only I could get to it and use it to effect.

The prospect of certain death was a powerful tonic. I bounded, zigzagging across the room, more Nijinsky than Dempsey, and that vicious fizzling sound erupted again. Its aim was improving. In spite of my disparate evasions, the leather thong holding the axe parted inches from my fingers, and I snatched it out of the air.

The genie, or whatever the shadow-thing would be properly termed, was invulnerable to any physical assault. But perhaps it depended somewhat on the green star, the "lamp" that housed and perhaps sustained it. I directed my attention to that. As to whether something that had endured a million years in the Antarctic would be susceptible to human agency, I did not know. But as Sergeant Eagleton would say, "Just hit him as hard as you can, Gunner Stubbs; he's only human"—though of course in this case, that hardly applied.

I ducked low, moving from side to side. The thing loomed in front of me like a clot of shadows blocking my way. With a cry, I ran right through it, raised the ice axe, and with a powerful double-handed blow brought its point down on the green star. It was a bold move, and perhaps the spirit of Sir Ernest rewarded my boldness. An inch on either side and I should have missed entirely, but the steel point landed squarely on the centre of the star as momentum carried me forward and over it. I rolled and struck the desk, expecting each instant to hear that hiss again, scanning to see where the shadow thing was.

It was gone as abruptly as it had come.

A faint green haze surrounded the ice axe embedded deep in the floorboards. There was no other sign of the green stone, save for a faint star-shaped imprint in the floor where it had been driven in before it burst. The only sound was my heavy breathing as I clambered to my feet.

"Bravo," said Mrs Crawford in a faint voice. She was lying where she had fallen. Blood had spread around her like a dark rug.

"I'll fetch a doctor."

"Please—don't leave me."

I kneeled awkwardly next to her. She reached out, and I took her hand. It was cold.

"I am so sorry. To have put you to so much trouble. Harcourt was much worse than I thought. Madder. Mad enough to try to wake Them. Thank God you averted that."

"Those things you and he were saying. Were they true?"

"Mostly." She swallowed. "I'm afraid I deceived you again. False promises of riches... I am glad you survived after all." She swallowed again with more difficulty. "Please don't cry now. I've done bad things. This is - poetic justice." She looked up at the ceiling. I thought she was not going to speak again, but she was composing herself for a final statement. The words, when they came, were a whisper. "You did very well, Mr Stubbs. Thank you."

Then I was left all alone. Alone, kneeling in blood, with the dead around me.

EPILOGUE

AND THAT IS THE STORY of how Harry Stubbs claimed victory in what was, by any measure, the most unusual bout he ever contested. I was not as unscathed as I thought. Arthur Renville pointed out that I had lost half an ear, sliced off as clean as you like, with a furrow I had never even felt ploughed in my temple.

Of course, I called on Arthur to help pick up the pieces. Who else would know what to do? He was angry at first, but the pile of cash on Harcourt's desk helped smooth matters over. He listened to my story, and by the end he had his feet up on the desk and was smoking one of Harcourt's cigars. He was satisfied the whole affair was over and things could return to normal. His verdict was that Connell and Harcourt would not be missed, and it seems he was right. I cannot say how much of my story he believed.

As for Mrs Crawford, or whatever her real name was, nobody came looking for her either. The woman I saw in the office was just a role she put on and took off as easily as I remove my bowler hat. But I don't suppose I'd ever have had any answers from her, even if she had lived.

Things did carry on as normal. The world is still the same. But my understanding of what is normal has changed. Before, I thought I understood everything. But now the world is too much for me, now I have seen how much I never understood at all and never will. Once I thought Shackleton was a hero. Now I see he was a hero and a fool, and a hero again, and six other things besides.

So many other people are living lives beyond me. Even as I write, Frank Mellors is in his antique shop in Chichester, showing an amethyst brooch to a customer. The men speak no special words, but there is a secret understanding between them. Another man in the shop looking at chinaware notices nothing.

A thousand miles away, Nanook of the North is cutting a hole in the ice to catch fish, a task as ordinary to him as opening a tin of pilchards is to you or me. I used to think such worlds as Nanook's only existed for as long as we watched them on the cinema screen. Now I realise many other worlds, and others that we have yet to dream of, are going on at the same time as our own, everywhere, even under our noses.

On the roof slates above my head, the tardigrades push their way through the moss. The little monsters pursue their prey and avoid predators as they have these six hundred million years, heedless of mankind's existence. Billions and billions of them, on all our roofs and in every park and garden, whole empires of tardigrades, and only a few like Dr Evans know they are even there.

Ten thousand miles south, the Ancients' tombs are still undisturbed, thousands of feet beneath the elder ice. The Ancients themselves are not dead but passing a few more millennia in dreamless, blank slumber until the world is right for them again. We human beings scurry about, oblivious to their presence.

We are not the Earth's favoured first-born, the inheritors of the world, as we had always imagined. We are the second-born and here only on the sufferance of our elder brothers. Though to them, we are much less than brothers. We are the tardigrades on the roof, the rats in the walls. We think we own the place, but it is only ours until they wake again. We are pets to them, or else we are vermin. Some time ago, they gave their chosen ones rings, like the collar on a pet dog, so they would not kill them by accident. Because the rest of us are nothing more than pests, a threat to their valuables. And their mousetraps are deadly effective.

It is not easy to see mankind relegated so low, so that even Harcourt only hoped to trail behind the Ancients. Perhaps that was why Armydale shot himself after coming back from the *Endurance* expedition. Perhaps he had seen the size of the world compared to us, and it was too much for him.

As for Harry Stubbs, well, another of his dreams has slipped away like the others. I was never going to be a master butcher like my father. I was never going to face Dempsey in front of a packed house at Madison Square Garden. And now I was never going to be an articled clerk with a respectable job in a solicitor's office. But if I learned anything from Sir Ernest Shackleton, it was the importance of picking yourself up after each setback. You must change course and start heading for the next dream. It might be only another Fata Morgana, but it keeps you going. And it might be real.

My reports, written with so much care for Mr Rowe, are no more. But I wish to record *my* story. Perhaps we will learn the same secrets as the Ancients, and our science will scale the same heights. Perhaps in a hundred years we too will make glowing lamps you can hold in your hand, lamps that can do all the things Mrs Crawford said. Then a man will be able to summon up a whole library with a gesture, and read it all, and make sense of it all at last. And maybe Harry Stubbs' story will be one of the books in that library.

If you enjoyed this story, why not post a review on Amazon? You'll be helping others discover a new writer and share the pleasure.

Or visit the Shadows from Norwood Facebook page –

https://www.facebook.com/ShadowsFromNorwood

For links, photographs, interactive map and more about the writing of the stories that comprise the Norwood Necronomicon.

Coming in 2015 from PS Publishing: The Dulwich Horror and Others, *a collection of seven stories of mystery and horror*

Lightning Source UK Ltd.
Milton Keynes UK
UKOW04f0039150716

278454UK00017B/444/P